Tessie Gillis

Stories *from* *the* Woman *from* Away

Tessie Gillis

Stories *from the* Woman *from* Away

Breton Books
Wreck Cove, Cape Breton Island
1996

Copyright © 1996 Helena Gillis MacLeod

Breton Books
Wreck Cove, Nova Scotia B0C 1H0

Production Assistance: Bonnie Thompson
Composition: Glenda Watt. Design: Ron Caplan. The cover is a composite of photos by Warren Gordon, Ray Martheleur and Tessie Gillis, by Artplus.

Publisher's Note: Throughout this book, Tessie Gillis has used "ye" to convey the spoken form of "you" as it often sounds in Cape Breton. It is not the "ye" of Shakespeare which rhymes with "glee," but rather a sound close to "yeah," but much shorter.

The Gaelic greeting "Ciamar a tha sibh?" ("How are you?") is written here as it often sounds to English ears—"Cummina Hashen!" And, "bodach" is Gaelic for "old man" or "stingy old man," but it's often used with friendliness and warmth.

This first edition is a work of fiction, based on the final manuscript by Tessie Gillis, edited with Evelyn Garbary. Portions of some chapters appeared in 1992 in *The Promised Land*, edited by James Taylor, published by Wilf Cude, Medicine Label Press.

Canadian Cataloguing in Publication Data

Gillis, Tessie, 1910-1972
   Stories from the woman from away
   ISBN 1-895415-15-2
I. Title.

PS8563.I513S86 1996   C813'.54   C96-950048-8
PR9199.3.G45S86 1996

Contents

Last Chapter But One   *1*

The Road to Elysium   *25*

The Glen   *38*

Our New Home   *63*

The Children   *79*

Our First Christmas   *91*

Gothic Neighbours   *103*

Dave   *106*

The Raid on the Promised Land   *111*

The Day the Men Went to Town   *139*

The Funeral   *155*

**This book is dedicated to the memory of
Evelyn Garbary
Tessie's friend and first editor**

Last Chapter But One

SINCE EARLY SUMMER the dust on the roads has been raised by cars with American licence plates. There were visitors in every house and callers began their rounds as soon as they had recovered from the previous night's festivities.

Most of the people who called were strangers to me. They called to see Jim. Entertaining was hard work and required a great deal of ingenuity since no one ever went to the grocers more than twice a month. I made endless molasses cookies and threw in oats to take the place of flour. I used stale bread and dried fruit to make puddings no one had ever heard of let alone tasted before. I used up most of my homemade cheese. Meat was the problem. Jim had butchered a cow and a pig for winter, but the barrels had been empty for months. There were only chickens left and they were going fast. I skipped many meals. The children were neglected I know, and there seemed to be no end to the stream of visitors.

The Highland Games were on and we had all been invited. Jim had taken the children down to his father's place to make the final arrangements. The house was empty! I locked the door, and placed the washtub in the middle of the kitchen floor. I would take a bath. The first this summer. If only I didn't feel so tired I'd be happy. Thank God there wouldn't be any teas to prepare today. There would be time to talk to the children—to listen to what they had to say.

I gave myself a good soaping...it was lovely feeling so fresh and clean. It was hard to get out of the water. I didn't seem to have the strength to pull myself up. "I look like a plucked chicken—only yellow. It must be worse than I thought." (I had taken to talking to myself for some time now.) I walked over to the sink and took down the little mirror from the nail on the wall. My eyes were hollow, my skin the colour of parchment and stretched taut over pointed bones that threatened to perforate the transparent skin. I had no hips and sagging skin hung in bags where my buttocks had been. I looked down at my breasts. I cupped the bags of empty skin that only months ago had been firm flesh.

"Jim can't have noticed. I'll tell him I have to see a doctor.... The kids are so small. What'll happen to them? I won't tell him today. Today is their big day...and they shall enjoy it if it kills me. I'll tell Jim tomorrow."

I looked across the fields. I had been across those fields all day, yesterday, the day before, and the day before. "It's over-ripe. All the good'll be gone out of it if it isn't cut soon." Two weeks now...

for two weeks I've been chasing animals out of that hay. If Jim doesn't fix that break in that fence today I'll go down myself and fix it some way...fifteen for dinner and only six plates and six cups (three without handles)...plenty of tea but no meat. Who ever tried to feed fifteen on two pounds of meat? Cut it small and make plenty of gravy, then fill them up with bread.... No use talking to Jim unless I catch him early in the morning and even then he can't think of anything but his thick head.

"I wish to hell they'd all go home," Jim said as he got into bed that night. "I wuz down the road lookin' today. The hay should'a been cut a week ago, an' the fence is down in the upper corner."

"I know," I said.

Jim had declined an invitation to go to a dance at Beatons' that evening and had found the strength to resist all the pleading and protestations that followed. I slept that night but before dawn a car pulled into the yard. The horn sounded sharp staccato blasts. At first Jim refused to stir, but soon the noise became painful to hear and he leapt out of bed and ran down the stairs in his bare feet. I staggered over to the window. Two young men were seated in a flashy new convertible. They had come to show off their new car. Symbol of success! A golden-winged Thunderbird. Jim didn't invite them into the house or offer them a drink.

"Thank you, God!" I whispered, as the roar of the engine died away and the dust on the road slowly subsided.

Jim stayed up and went out to water the horse. Yes, the hay would be cut today! I was sitting down enjoying a cup of coffee, the children were out playing and the house was quiet when four men drove up the road, past the house, and stopped at the field where Jim was working. I watched them as they got out of the car, opened the trunk and took out a bottle. Two of the men took off their jackets, but the other two could hardly stand up and did not attempt such a difficult task in spite of the heat of the sun.

It wasn't long before Lauchie and Harold Beaton came down the road, and J.J. and Dougall came up the hill. Many more bottles appeared from the trunk of the car. Three staggering figures followed the hay-rack round the field with forks on their shoulders unable to lift a straw. Three slept under a tree at the edge of the field. Somehow the hay was cut and all but the last load stowed safely in the barn. Then I noticed one of the men glance at his watch. I saw Jim shake his head—they all started to plead with him. At last Jim got in the car after leaving instructions with Lauchie about stacking the last load.

THAT NIGHT A HEAVY FROST covered the countryside. Autumn was in the air although summer had barely cast a shadow. Here and there, in the woods, the young maples turned crimson and blazed a warning no one could ignore. Reluctantly the visitors took their leave of families and friends.

Everyone went back to work with relief.

"What makes ye so yellow?" said Jim one evening as though seeing me for the first time.

"Are you just noticing? Didn't you even notice how black I looked in those pictures at the Highland Games?"

"No!" Jim could be terse when reminded of his behaviour in the past, especially when he didn't know what the implication might be.

"I'm sick, Jim. Can't you see how awful thin I am? All summer long it's been all I could do to get out of bed in the mornings."

"Do ye think ye should see a doctor?"

"If I'm going to stay on my feet I'd better see one." I couldn't stop the tears now. "Jim, can't you SEE?"

"All right! All right!" Jim snapped back, but he looked at me for a long while.

All that fall I tended a doctor. He couldn't locate my trouble on the first visit or on the many visits that followed. He would go to his cupboard, look over the rows of bottles solemnly and each time take down a different one.

"Try this, Mrs. Douglas?" he would say and "Come back in two weeks time."

I came to enjoy my visits to the doctor. I made many friends in his waiting room, but Ellen Cameron I came to love. We began exchanging notes. Ellen knew she was taking nerve pills, and I had just been given the same ones. Five of my neighbours had come into town with me. Some wanted to visit the grocer and some the vendor. We had agreed to meet at Ellen's place. While Ellen was getting tea ready I noticed how stiff her body seemed to be and how tightly she clenched her fists as she stood at the range.

"Come on," I said, "we'd better go, it'll be getting dark soon." No one made a move.

"Ye must stay and hev some tea," said Charlie, Ellen's husband, as he put his hand on his wife's shoulder. "You're all right now, aren't ye, honey?"

A rumble of voices drowned my protests. Ellen made the tea. I couldn't take my eyes off her face. The men were drinking beer and they were laughing. At last I managed to persuade the others to leave. That was the last time I saw Ellen alive. It was Janice Lawlor who brought the news.

"Dead! Ellen?"

Janice rushed over to stop me from falling. She helped me into a chair.

"Someone must have the names mixed up," I whispered. "I was with her only last week." This was all I could say. I couldn't believe it. Ellen was only forty. Five years younger than I was. It was not until I saw Ellen in her coffin that I could believe that she was dead. Charlie couldn't tell me anything. He could only stare before him. There were no tears in his eyes. I grabbed Jim's arm.

"Come on, Jim," I said, "I want to stop at Ellen's mother's place. There is something I have to know."

Jim drove me to the farm where Ellen had

been raised. A girl of twelve sat in the rocker beside the stove in the kitchen, a baby on her knee. I drew up a chair and sat down beside her.

"How did she die?" I asked. "She couldn't have been sick long?"

"NO!" the girl replied, "not long. They took her to Halifax."

"Halifax! What happened? Was it sudden?"

"It was to Dartmouth—to the mental home, they wuz after takin' 'er to. Ellen got a pain one night, an' he took 'er upstairs to bed. When Charlie got home he called the doctor. But Ellen wouldn't talk to the doctor, so he gave her a needle and left. Daddy came home and sent Mama down to help." The girl stopped—she remembered she was talking to a stranger.

"Well, what happened then? Please tell me?"

"Well, I'll tell ye all I can. The doctor came ag'in next mornin' with herself after bein' jist like that all night and still not lettin' on she heard anybody at all. Doctor Angus gave 'er another needle an' told Mama, 'She jist won't talk. She could answer questions if she wanted to. It's jist 'er nerves. I gave 'er somethin' to quiet 'er. She'll be all right.' Mama was awful mad. Ellen layin' there, nothin' but skin an' bone like she wuz, an' him sayin' nothin' wuz wrong."

"Then what happened?"

"Well, they took 'er to the mental hospital, only they said it was to a hospital in Halifax she wuz goin' to."

"What did the doctor tell Charlie, do you know?"

"No! But mebbe a week after Ellen took the pain, he told Charlie there wasn't nothin' the matter with 'er, that he could only keep on givin' 'er needles. He said fer Charlie to send 'er, or take 'er up to the mental hospital for a few treatments. Ellen was still layin' in bed. So Charlie took 'er up in the car." The girl shifted the baby on to her other knee. "Ellen let Mama dress 'er, then she walked to the door, not lookin' to right or left, past th' kids an' all. The only time she showed she knowed any o' them was to put 'er hand on the baby's head when she passed by th' high chair. She didn't talk none though."

That was all she knew. I had to wait until the funeral to learn the rest. They had given Ellen "treatment" at the mental hospital. The following morning she ate her breakfast, talked to the nurses and seemed better. Charlie started on the seven-hour journey home. When he arrived there was a telegram for him—"Hurry back. We need your permission to operate." Charlie grabbed a bite to eat and sped back to the hospital. Before he had been admitted to the room Ellen was dead.

THAT WAS LAST YEAR. Another summer has come and gone. We still had many visitors, but now they were chiefly neighbours, their relations and acquaintances. The visits all began the same way. The man would pull a bottle out of his pocket and say he had come to treat Jim, but I was the one they had come to see. I knew that. Their scrutiny made me feel uncomfortable and I tried to escape to the kitchen as soon as politeness permitted. Their warmth and concern was unbearable. Angus and Mary Gillis came out from town; Peter and Jane Campbell from the glen on the other side of the mountain; the MacLeods, the Sullivans and the Kavanaghs from the Irish settlement. I hadn't been near a doctor since Ellen died. I no longer had the strength to finish a batch of bread and the churning was more than I could handle; Jim had to take over the dasher as soon as the butter began to form, and if he went out of the house I had to leave the churn the way it was until he returned. I caught cold.

"I don't know what's the matter, Jim, every once in a while I get an awful pain in my chest."

"I coughed all night meself!" said Jim. "It's goin' around. Everybody's down with it."

The cold left but the cough stayed. Then one night I woke up ringing wet, there were big drops of sweat on my forehead. I sat on the edge of the bed and rested my arms on my knees. Drops of sweat fell to the floor.

Jim took me to a doctor on the other side of the Island.

"Mrs. Douglas, I can't find anything wrong with your heart. You don't need to worry about that. I'll give you some cough medicine, take a tablespoon every four hours."

"Seven dollars for nothing but a bottle of cough medicine," I said to Jim as we climbed back into the truck. "But he did say my heart was good. That's all I wanted to know. Long as my heart is good I can throw anything off."

I seemed to have added strength for a while after that, maybe because of what the doctor had said. I started to clean the house, but my pain didn't go away and my new-found energy didn't last for long. I gave up taking the medicine. When the callers came I could only give them cookies with their tea—no more cakes and pies.

One day Blaze and Peggy MacLellan called. They hadn't been to the house for over two years. I made tea for them and stayed in the room until Blaze and Jim started telling stories, then I escaped into the kitchen. Soon Blaze came out after me carrying his cup and plate.

"Dear heart, thank ye," he said, putting his dishes down on the kitchen table, "I couldn't eat a bite." He came over to me and put his arm around my shoulder. "I'm sorry to see ye under the weather." I tried to edge away but Blaze wouldn't let me move. "I hope ye don't hold it against me for stayin' away so long. I'm sorry."

"Quit worrying," I said. I managed to throw off his arm and staggered into the living room. "Jim, you'd better give Blaze a drink. Get the bottle!"

They didn't stay long after that.

"Don't you think it's funny that Peggy and Blaze looked us up?" I said to Jim, after they had gone. "Making the excuse of going to Mass in the

Glen when they've passed us by time after time for two years?"

"What are ye dreamin' up now?"

"Well, Blaze was lolligagging over me in the kitchen. I couldn't make out what he was talking about but he was trying to apologize for something. He kept after me like he couldn't rest until he was forgiven."

"Yer imaginin' things."

"No, I'm not, Jim. And it's not only Blaze but all those people we've had visiting. People we hardly know except to pass the time of day with. You haven't been telling around that I'm sick, have you?"

"I suppose I did mention it, but what's wrong with that?"

"Now I can feel sorry for your poor father."

"What's he got to do with it?"

"Those two weeks before he died. Lying there, conscious, not able to talk, but understanding every word, and people from all over the Island flocking in like vultures. He knew...he knew."

"Knew what? What kind of talk is that? Talk sense if you want me to listen to you."

"Jim! They all think I'm going to die. That's why they're coming. They think I'm going to die."

IT WAS ON A SATURDAY late in February, I remember. The Glen was buried in snow. The winding trail to the highway twisted up and down the hills between high cliffs of snow. Saturdays were always busy days for me, and this Saturday was particularly so. The ladies of the parish were holding a fund-raising card party for the church and I had promised to bake for them. I had the last batch of cakes in the oven when I felt a sharp pain in my back. I thought that a five-minute rest would relieve it, so I went into the other room and sat down in the big old upholstered chair. The pain eased in no time at all.

There was still the churning to be done for I had no butter for the sandwiches. I had only made a few turns with the handle when the pain struck again—this time in the chest. I managed to slide into the nearest chair. Jim was reading the paper before the fire and the children were playing in the other room. Once again the pain almost disappeared; once again I went back to my work, but this time when the pain returned it was like an iron claw—a grappling hook, and it seemed to be pulling outwards as though trying to burst through my ribs. Flames of pain shot up into my throat and down my arms. I tried to call out—but there was no air to breathe. I felt I was breathing cotton candy. I managed to reach the staircase, climb the stairs and reach my bed. Lying down only made the pain worse. I tried to call Jim, but he didn't answer. I tried again.

"What do you want?" Jim answered. I listened for his footsteps on the stairs.

"Jim! Get the priest," I called. This time Jim heard me and came running up the stairs.

"Git the priest? What's the matter? Don't you feel good?"

"It's my heart. Get the priest."

"Mary, ye can't mean that. Ye were all right a minute ago. Lay down on the pillow." Jim tried to push me down. "Rest a while. Ye don't want a priest, do ye? It can't be yer heart...."

"Maybe it's not my heart." I couldn't keep my eyes open any longer. "Maybe it's pneumonia or something."

"I'll go git the priest, if ye want.... It isn't your heart, Mary, is it? Are ye sure? It can't be.... Yer jist tired."

"I guess so."

I couldn't help thinking of the children. I wanted to be with them at the end. After a little while I asked Jim to help me down the stairs. He lifted me from stair to stair. Somehow I managed to reach my favourite chair by the old Quebec heater. The children knew at once that something was wrong. Anne found an old hot water bottle. Sonny brought me a pillow. The pain wasn't so bad when I sat quiet and didn't talk. The steel claws relaxed their hold and the burning ache was almost a relief. But how was I going to convince Jim of the need for help?

There was a knock on the door. It was Dougall come to collect the cakes and cookies for the church party. Dougall did not have to be told. In twenty minutes he had returned with J.J. and his pick-up truck. Jim and the children searched for my clothes, but I could not raise my arms, so they had to throw the coat over my shoulders. Jim and Dougall helped me out the back door and lifted me into the truck.

The school yard was full of cars and trucks. The whole community had gathered for the party. Surely there would be one car fit to drive along the highway! A car with headlights and brakes fit to drive twenty-eight miles.

"I'll be back in a minute," said Jim, "are ye warm enough?"

I nodded and watched Jim as he went over to a car across the yard. The driver had just started up the engine—he was an old friend. Jim bent down and talked to him, then I could see the driver pointing to another car. The pain got worse and I had to clench my teeth to keep from screaming. Jim was lost in the shadow but now it didn't seem to matter.... Where were the children? Were they still in the back of the truck in this wind? I could see Jim running from one car to another. It was the old story, one had no gas, and there were no gas stations open at this hour.... Another's brakes were gone and the roads were too icy to take a chance. The MacDonalds had a car full of passengers and were afraid they wouldn't have a way home. Every one had an excuse. I could see Jim coming back to the truck.

"No one will go with us," he said. "I've asked everyone I know."

"Let's go home, Jim, I'm cold. We won't get away."

"No! Now we're here I'll find someone." Jim tried to tuck the coat around my neck. "Are ye all right till I get back? I'll try again."

At last Jim understood. In a short time he came running back.

"John Angus is goin' to go with us. Be here in a minute. Gone to tell the crowd he came with to wait at Dougall's fer 'im."

I tried to raise myself up.

"No! No! Don't stir. Ye'd best wait till 'e drives over. 'Tis bitter cold in the wind."

John Angus was kind and considerate. From time to time I could see him taking his eyes off the road to look at me.

"How are ye?" he said. "Can ye stand it? The roads are rough where th' slush froze in the ruts."

At last we reached the highway and I thought we would be able to make better time, but the plow had only cleared a single track and the banks of snow were higher than a man's head. John Angus drove as though unaware of danger.

"It's not so bad," he said. "If there's a rig comin' I can see the lights once in a while on th' top of th' drifts."

But the car coming to meet us only had one headlight working and the driver and his companion had been drinking. John Angus thrust his foot down on the brake and waited for the impact. Thank God, the other driver crashed into the snow on his left. I supposed I could only have been barely conscious, for I felt no sense of relief when the danger had passed. We only met one other car in the remaining twenty miles, but John Angus saw it coming, found a turnoff, and waited until it had passed.

It was ten-thirty when we drove up the drive to the hospital and parked beside the doctor's house. The doctor's car wasn't there.

"The doctor's out on a call," his wife said. "He should be back any minute, if you'll wait."

We waited in the car. Soon twin ribbons of light pierced the darkness. It was the doctor. I told him my story.

I HEARD MYSELF SCREAM. I must have been in a deep sleep.... I felt as though my body was crumbling into a fine grain and floating up from my feet into my fingers...into my head. The seeds of life were gathering there...waiting...ready to float away....

"Mary!" I knew it was the doctor's voice. "Mary! Would you like a priest? I don't want to scare you. I'll keep trying. I'll not give up. But if you want a priest, Nurse will call him right away."

"Yes!" I managed to whisper.

"O God! If only I could stay with my children for a few years longer...until they no longer need me...then I shall be happy to go, if it is thy will."

The hospital called Jim that morning at the number he had written on the admittance sheet, but the people who had the telephone lived three miles away and they didn't take the message to him until nine o'clock that night.

FOR EIGHT WEEKS I lay there being fed, washed and tended by nurses, but the pain and the burning ache never went away. "It isn't your heart, Mary, that is causing the pain," the doctor said. "Your heart is coming along well. The infarction mended well. It's your arteries, you have hardening of the arteries."

That was wonderful news. My heart is coming along well, that's what the doctor said. That is all that matters. The pain will go away if only I could get out of this bed and walk around. Every day I asked the doctor the same question. Every day he would shake his head. After many weeks he looked at me and smiled.

"I suppose I'll be a little weak when I first get up," I said with a laugh, "but I'll bounce right back like a rubber ball, you'll see. I'll just stay here for a few days—go to the bathroom, maybe, then tomorrow I'll go visiting the women in the ward,"

That was the way I thought it would be. But after a week I was only able to take three steps over to the dresser, and I was able to crawl back into bed. It was not until the hundredth day that I had the courage to ask the doctor if I could go home.

"Can you dress yourself, Mary?" he asked.

"Oh, yes, doctor, and I can walk as far as the Nursery. I've been going to see the babies every day."

"Well, maybe you would be better off with your family," he said. "But remember, there'll always be a bed here for you."

That doctor was a fine man.

I went home the next day. The children gave me a great welcome. I told Jim I would have to rest that evening, but I'd fix up the house a little the next morning.

"Are ye crazy?" said Jim. "The doctor said you're not to do anythin'."

The next morning when the children had gone to school and Jim had gone into the woods, I got up and went into the kitchen. I thought it would be nice to make some biscuits. I went into the pantry. What a mess! Dishes were scattered all over the counter. The mixing bowl wasn't in the cupboard, it had been put on a shelf—dirty. The pan wasn't hanging on the wall—it was under a pile of other pans on the floor.

Slowly I went to work. I put more wood on the fire, washed the bowl and the pan. Then I rested, gripped my chest and tried to breathe deeply. I measured the flour and mixed the ingredients in the bowl. Very slowly I cut the biscuits and placed the pan in the oven and crept back into bed. Jim hadn't gone into the woods after all, he had only gone down to the barn.

"What in the name of God is in the oven?" he said as he opened the kitchen door. "Hev ye been up?"

"I tried to make a pan of biscuits," I said. "Leave me alone, Jim, until this pain goes."

The pain didn't go and I had to go back to the hospital.

"'The cat came back at the hour of four,'" sang a jolly nurse. "Can't stay away from us now, can you?"

Three times I had to return to the hospital before I came to know that there was only one place for me in my own home and that was in bed. All I could do was think, look around—and call the children.

"Anne! Come here and bring the broom. Look at the dust under the table; at the cobwebs over there in the corner. Can't you see? You never saw things this way when I was up. The rest of you act as if you didn't see dirt. Maybe you don't, and I could have saved myself all that slaving just to keep the house clean for everyone. Nobody ever noticed, I guess."

"Oh! Mama!" Anne was nearly in tears now.

"What if I die tonight and the neighbours come to get ready for the wake. Wouldn't you care if the house was dirty?"

Then I would lie looking out of the window and watch the cattle going to water. The old red cow was about to calf. I called Jim.

"Jim, aren't you going to look at that cow before you go to bed?"

"No!" he said. "Why? She ain't gonna calf for two, three weeks yet. You an' them sons o' whores cows!"

I waited for Sonny to come in.

"Sonny! Come here to me," I called. "I want you to take a flashlight and go out and take a look at that old red cow for me."

"What fer, Mama? I don't want to go, she ain't goin' to calf."

"Sonny! Now you take that flashlight and get out to the barn. Take Anne with you if you're afraid."

Sonny slammed out of the room and I could hear him putting on his boots noisily in the kitchen. Then I heard Jim's voice.

"What's wrong? Where are you goin' this time o' night?"

"Oh! I hev to go an' look at that darned cow. Mama made me."

"Her an' them bastard cows. Thet cow ain't goin' to calf for three weeks."

"Thet's what I told 'er, but she made me go anyway."

I heard the door slam behind Sonny.

I KEPT THE BLINDS PULLED DOWN after that. One day I heard the clatter of breaking china and glass. I closed my eyes and put my hands to my ears. The only pieces of glass and china in the pantry were old and cherished. Sonny ran into the room.

"Mama! Anne dropped a whole pile of dishes and broke 'em all!"

"Don't holler so loud, Sonny, I can hear you. What dishes did Anne break?"

"Your good ones, Mama."

I looked at him. His eyes were open wide.

"The red bowl you put the oranges an' apples

in at Christmas, an' the little glass dishes with the flowers made right in 'em, an' the big platter."

"I had the bowl ever since my mother died, and she had it long before I can remember." I tried to keep my voice steady. "Anne should have been more careful. I had those things for over twenty years. Some of them were my mother's wedding gifts."

"She's always breakin' things." Sonny looked scornfully at Anne crying in the doorway.

"Sonny, keep quiet. Here, come here, dear." I held out my arms to the little twelve-year-old girl. "Come now, dry your eyes. But you must be more careful, what will we eat out of when all the dishes are broken? There, there, everything will be all right."

TWO MONTHS PASSED and there were many changes in the house and on the farm. I had learned to accept them all without saying a word. It was like being dead and seeing all I had worked for wasted and destroyed. I was helpless to lift a finger and change anything. Once in a while, maybe on a dry and windy day, my spirits would rally and I would not be able to control myself. It happened when Lauchie told me he would be coming to help Jim butcher the next day.

"What are you butchering?" I had asked the question without stopping to think.

"The brown cow!" Jim replied.

"The brown cow! Are you foolish? She's the

biggest cow we have and has the nicest calves of them all. Why don't you butcher one of those runts? Butcher Nellie."

"There wouldn't be enough meat on 'er to bother takin' to town. Besides that brown bastard's goin' through all th' fences."

"Jim!" I couldn't stop myself now. "We had seventeen head of cattle when I got sick, and you've got them down to seven now. What's the matter with you? If you sell that big cow and keep those runts you'll have nothing but runts in a couple of years. De-horn the brown cow—but keep her. She's mine. Your mother gave her to me when she was a calf. Please don't butcher her."

The brown cow was saved, but the cursing and grumbling from the kitchen went on for days. I often cried. I couldn't help myself. At first I thought the children were frightened to see tears in my eyes but soon they became indifferent.

A YEAR PASSED. It was fall again. One night the house was very quiet, but I couldn't sleep. "Everything has gone," I said to the darkness. "Everything but Jim and the children. But who am I to doubt God's wisdom? Who am I indeed?" Shapes began to form in the darkness...words rang in my ears...sounds out in the night became louder...the wind playing tag in the branches of the old willow...a fox barking at some unseen creature. "What does it matter if generations of spiders flourish in the corners of my living room?" I leaned over, switched on the light, opened the drawer in the table beside the bed and took out a writing pad and pencil. Words were tumbling over and over in my mind.... I picked up the pencil and began to write....

Blustering, on the eve of All Saints, winter sheds its first snow, a lace that vanishes overnight. A warning to man and beast to prepare. It asks of man—"Is your harvest in? The oats, the hay, the feed for the herd? The potatoes, the cabbage, the turnips and all? Are they dug and stored in your cellar, warm and dry? Is your house patched up against the wind, and banked round the sills where the cold seeps in? Have you harnessed your horses and gathered the maple, the long white birch and the occasional ash, cut in the hot months of summer against the time when the woods will be waist-deep with snow, and boughs bent down and saddened with their heavy load? Is your barn mended? The roof all patched against the winter when the dampness will try the best it can to seep inside and blacken the hay? Hay that should the animals eat in their hunger, would make them sicken and perhaps die? Have you sawed, chopped, and stacked the winter logs in some sheltered place where drifts won't bury them so deep that only an axe can free them? Have you located your animals every one?"

The animals leave the distant feeding grounds, and by instinct come back to last year's habitation. Chained or roped, with freedom gone, they yet have daily food of sorts there, that quiets the rumble of empty paunches. Here, there is no thirst for days on end with only snow to wet their throats, but clean clear water from a spring at the end of a shoveled path.

"Have you found that heifer that stayed with the green of the undergrowth in the stand of fir and spruce, and led her home again to the safety of her stall?"

Then the voices of winter, bellowing, raging, mourning and sorrowful, in turn, can do their utmost. You are ready!

Blowing snow, ice-laden branches, giant drifts shifting from place to place, now here, now there, like pebbles skipped by a child on the sea, what do you care? The nights, when the rafters groan and strain and you wonder why they do not split from their studdings. The dawn, cold and forbidding, breaking on a whitened world, when there is no trace of man or beast to break the stillness. Northern windows, darkened by drifting snow, blot out the shrouded, weighted woods, trees bent in thanksgiving....

The Road to Elysium

IT WAS SO HOT IN NEW YORK that the leaves rattled on the trees and the city had a dusty look of a house long unused.

"Jim, let's not go back to work right away."

"O.K. If we get fired we can always get work some place else."

"We could take another month off? Let's go where it's cool."

"Let's go home!" said Jim as if his native place had been in his thoughts ever since he left there, twenty years ago.

"Well, don't you think it's time you took me to meet your folks? We've been married four years."

We had only been back in New York half an hour and our suitcases, still unpacked, stood in the middle of the living room. The journey from Oakville, Montana, had been long, the train hot and airless; but it had been a wonderful vacation, back home—the country—the farm—the animals.

"We'd best take some warm clothing, it's always cool in Cape Breton," said Jim, picking up the telephone.

I couldn't believe it. I dumped my suitcase on the bed and started unpacking.

"Don't bother to tidy up," said Jim, slamming the telephone. "There's not much time."

In less than half an hour we were in a taxi driving under the Hudson River and on our way to Penn Station and looking for a northbound train. We were both over thirty and should have had more sense.

We passed through miles of muslin-covered tobacco fields in Maine and were only aware that we had passed into Canada by the presence of excise men passing along the coaches. It wasn't until we reached Truro, two hundred miles from the border, that I noticed how different the people were. I noticed that I was the only woman wearing high heels and that Jim was the only man bare-headed. The men were wearing long-billed caps, out of style in the south. The women's clothing was sensible rather than fashionable. They either didn't care about their figures or their dieting didn't work. Their shoulders were narrow, breasts skimpy, their hips and legs heavy.

"I have some magazines, would you like to read them to pass the time?" The woman sitting opposite folded her calloused hands primly across the well-worn purse on her lap.

"No, thank you," she said without smiling.

"This is my first visit to Canada. Are you going to Cape Breton?"

"No!"

"The country is lovely, isn't it? Are you going far?"

"No!"

I didn't know which question she was answering. She won't even bother to find out whether she likes me or not, I thought to myself.

Jim sat there silently looking out of the window of the train, as if he had forgotten the beauty of his native land.

The ninety-seven miles from Truro took seven hours. Few travelled to Cape Breton and the railroad used its oldest coaches on the line. They had straight wooden backs and only the seats were padded. The ladies' room was so dirty that the only convenience I could use was the water cooler. The train stopped at every station. It was raining now. Hunched grey figures in drab coats and shabby footwear stood listlessly on the platform. I felt alone. Jim was the only person I knew in this vast country and he too seemed to be as remote as the landscape and the unsmiling faces on the platform.

"What's the matter?" said Jim, as I grabbed his arm.

"Nothing really...it's nothing," was all I could say.

Just then the steward came to the door of the coach.

"Last chance for the diner," he shouted, "first car ahead."

"I'm hungry," said Jim, "let's eat."

The diner was empty. There were four tables

covered with red and white chequered table cloths. An indifferent waiter sauntered over to our table and slapped down a menu. We had the choice of three courses. Two were fish and the third steak.

"I'm going to have that boiled salmon and steamed potatoes," said Jim, rubbing his hands. "You'd best try it too, never tasted anything till you've had boiled Atlantic salmon."

"Fish!" I couldn't hide my disgust. "I never heard of BOILED fish. I came from cattle people. I'll take the steak."

Jim ate his salmon with relish while I picked at a piece of steak that looked like leather dried in the sun. There were no vegetables.

"Doesn't anybody know about vegetables?" I ventured to ask.

"The only vegetables I had when I was growing up was cabbage and perhaps turnip. Carry-over from way back when the old-timers was too busy growing hay, grain, and potatoes. They didn't have time for gardens, I suppose."

The train began to slow down, we were pulling into a small town.

"Port Hawkesbury!" said Jim, as the train came to a halt.

"We have to change here. No hurry though. Has to wait for the 'up' train. There's our engine passing now." We rushed back to our seats, I fixed my hat (the ostrich feather had survived the journey) and grabbed my coat, purse and the smallest of our three suitcases. The train began to move.

"They're going to pull out!" I said in panic.

"No! No!" said Jim, pulling out our heavy case from under the seat. "They're only pulling up a bit to give the people in the back coach a chance to get off on the platform."

People were streaming off the train leaving their belongings strewn on the seats. The coach was nearly empty.

"Where is everyone going?" I asked.

"To the refreshment room," said Jim. "The train stays here a while."

The sun broke through the clouds as we stepped down on the platform. Our train went on to Sydney but we had to change to the "Inverness Flyer" as Jim called it. The station was crowded. Men and women milled about, the men shaking hands with friends, the women kissing and hugging relations or acquaintances in the waiting crowd. They all seemed to be laughing. Everyone was in a holiday mood. This was Canada as Jim had described it!

"Why wouldn't that woman on the train speak to me, Jim?"

"You'll have to get used to that. When they're ready, you'll find they'll talk. You might as well get used to that now. Come on! Our train's over there. We'd best shake a leg. Don't seem to be too many getting aboard."

On the side track at the rear of the train an engine snorted black smoke; a deep grumbling noise seemed to shake the boiler casting. It sounded like it had been waiting a long time and was now overtired. The tender was piled high with glistening coal. Next came the mail truck and baggage car with its single barred window. Two men sat at the entrance of the open doors, their legs dangling over the side. They stared at every passenger as they licked cigarette papers and rolled their cigarettes. There was no caboose and the train had a curious lopped-off appearance.

The step was high and I looked to see if anyone was watching before hiking my skirt above my knees. I must confess I felt out-of-place in my high-heeled patent leather shoes, neat black suit, white blouse with ruffles down the front and my black hat, feathers and all. So did Jim in his new brown suit with mirror-bright shoes to match. His shirt was glistening white and his wavy black hair shone in the sunlight.

"What are ye stoppin' for?" said Jim. "Let's get in where I can put down these suitcases. They're heavy."

The smell from the coach struck me like a blast of hot wind from the prairies. The coach seemed small because it had been divided into two compartments. The seats were placed like pews in a church. Their straight high backs and wooden seats were unpadded; only a penitent nun could find comfort on them. In the centre, a small pot-bellied stove squatted on a square of protective zinc like an over-stuffed toad. It bulged with candy wrappers, bottle caps, empty cigarette packages, paper bags, tobacco pouches, and whiskey wrappers. Spider webs hung in the corners from floor to ceiling. Dead flies and candy wrappers (faded dimmer than those in the stove) lay in the aisles and on the sills under the filthy windows. Beyond the stove and facing the last seat a ledge had been placed against the partition to serve as a desk. It was strewn with papers and a gaping satchel. This was obviously the conductor's seat.

"Pretty grim, ain't it?" said Jim. "Never noticed before."

"Hasn't been cleaned since it was built," was all I could find to say.

"It's mostly men who ride the train." Jim nodded towards the partition. "Women don't travel any."

The grain in the oak "pews" had been cut and polished with skill and infinite care. The wrought-iron lamp holder circling the hanging lamp hung drunkenly on a rusty chain from the ceiling, made of wrought iron and decorated with foliage of beaten bronze. Under a film of greasy soot the work of a fine craftsman was as unmistakable as beautiful features under a web of wrinkles on a woman's face. I stood tiptoe and tried to straighten it.

"Look out!" said Jim. "Ye'll get oil all over your clothes. It's still got some on the bottom. Must have been there a long time, judgin' from the colour. It's clear yellow."

"What a lamp!" I said. "I can just imagine it in some elegant parlour, all shined up till every petal of the flowers stands out. Filigree bronze. Why do you suppose anyone would put a thing so beautiful in a dirty place like this old coach?"

"Probably all they had when the railroad came in," said Jim. "Come on now, sit down before the conductor comes and thinks you're trying to steal it, or ye're gone off yer rocker. What's 'Filigree'?"

I chose a seat about half way down the coach. Jim dusted the seat carefully with his handkerchief before we sat down. In his own good time the conductor came and took our tickets.

"What did ye say yer name was?" he asked Jim.

"Douglas. Jim Douglas—from up the Glen."

"Oh yeh! Would ye be Austin Douglas' boy now?"

"No."

"Well, ye wouldn't be related to Alex Dougall, now would ye?"

The conductor went back to his place, shaking his head sadly. Jim watched the passengers come aboard.

"Do you think I could take a look into that compartment up there?" I asked.

"No! For God's sake, Mary! That's the smoker. There's men in there now!"

"How do you know?"

"I saw them come aboard."

The train lurched suddenly, the engine whistled and we started to rock along the tracks. The voices beyond the partition grew louder. Practiced fingers picked out the grace notes of an old Scottish tune. Feet stomped in time to the music.

"Come back on 'er, Angus!" a voice shouted.

"Good boy, Angus!" another shouted.

"I wonder if that man knows what a good violin he has?" I said. "If only he would put rosin on that bow!"

"Wait till you see how much talent there is up here," said Jim, grinning with pride, "I'll see that you 'take in' some dances."

I thought I had better clean up a little and went down to the door marked "Women." I opened the door and went inside. I looked down at the throne and saw the earth whizzing by between the sleepers. I did what I had to do. The wash basin was decorated with candy wrappers. I picked them up, it was almost a pity to disturb them, and since there was no waste basket, I threw them down the hole behind me. I turned on a tap—no water. I tried the other tap marked "hot"—no water. All I could do was make a face at the cracked mirror and pat my hair with dirty hands. I was very careful not to step backwards.

"Thought you were going to clean up?" Jim was laughing. I didn't dignify his question with an answer. By the time the train came to the next stop we were both laughing.

The train moved with incredible slowness. It took almost half an hour to reach the lonely little shack with "Timinitoul" painted on its side. This was a station. Two milk cans stood beside the tracks but there wasn't a soul in sight when the engine whistled to a stop. Then, like magic, men appeared from nowhere.

"How far are we from Port Hawkesbury?" I asked.

"Five miles, I guess. No more anyway," Jim answered.

"Only five miles! How far is it to the next station?"

"About thirty-five or thirty-eight miles. Ye'd best settle back for a long ride. The train's in no hurry. No schedule to keep. Any time it gets there's soon enough. Only goes to the other end of the county and stays there overnight."

The occupants of the smoker rushed off the train as soon as it stopped, taking their bottles with them. Soon passengers, local residents, conductors, engineer and brakeman mingled on the platform, passing the time of day, news, and bottles around. Each time a drink had been taken, a grimy hand brushed off the bottle top and passed it on to the next man, who did the same. Then someone noticed the little man with the violin.

"Cummina Hashen, Angus! Got yer fiddle with ye? How about givin' us a tune?" Angus needed no encouragement. He took one of the many bottles offered him, raised it to his lips, took a long drink and began to play.

"Give us a step, Duncan!" one of the men called out. A circle was formed and Duncan stepped forward to the rhythmic clapping of hands. After fifteen minutes or so the conductor must have realized the passage of time and shouted, "All aboard!" He shooed the passengers back into the train and dispatched the engineer to the engine.

It was the same at every stop. My seat grew harder. Before long a big, broad-shouldered fellow with sandy hair rocked out from the smoker. He staggered down the aisle with a quart bottle of beer grasped tightly in his hand. When he reached our seat he stopped and stared vacantly at Jim and then at me. I slid closer to Jim and stared back. Apparently satisfied that we didn't concern each other, the man resumed his journey down the aisle to the men's toilet.

"That was a wicked-looking one. Do you know him, Jim?"

"No. What are you afraid of? He was only trying to see if he could place me. See if he should give me a drink or not."

"Why is it they're all up there drinking and dancing and making all that noise?"

"It's on account of the liquor laws, I suppose," Jim answered. "Mabou and Inverness are the only places in the county that have liquor stores. It's agin' the law even to break the seals on the bottles until you get home. But it's a long way home for them. They must've been pretty dry to start so close to town. The conductor himself's in there, too, looks like."

All was quiet in the smoker for several minutes after the sandy-haired man got back.

"He's telling the others we're strangers," whispered Jim.

"Where did they come from back at the station? Out of the trees?"

"They were waiting special for the train. The mail driver was there, and the people livin' close by always come when the whistle blows—for news mostly. They come for a drink too."

At every crossroads and station, neighbours heard the whistle and came out to greet the train. Stops were frequent, and at each one, passengers, conductor, and engineer piled out and went through the same ritual.

"He better open her up," said Jim, "to make up time."

We had been rattling along at a fair speed since our last stop.

"WHAT WAS THAT?" I screamed, and clutched Jim's arm. The train took a great leap forward, gave a tremendous shudder, and stopped short.

"Must be the train gone off the tracks." Jim stood up and looked out of the window. "Used to do it regular in winter. Never heard of it in summer before." He chuckled, "Engineer had the old snail crowding the hare there at the last, did you notice?"

"What'll they do?" I moaned. "I'm so tired."

"Now, don't get upset. Good thing there's a crowd on the train. It won't take long to set her back on. Look out the window. Every man jack on the train's already out there. They'll have her back on the tracks in no time...if they can stand up long enough. Maybe we'd best go out too...I can see two or three of them won't be helpin' none."

Jim was right. Some could barely stand, some could only stagger. Two made it to the shade of the trees and went to sleep. Angus took out his fiddle and began to play. No one but Jim was steady on his feet, although the conductor and the engineer had been somewhat sobered by the jolt. It was Jim who set up the big jack and directed the use of it. The others (in tune to Angus' fiddle) made a frolic of hoisting up each car and pushing it back onto the rails. The job took an hour. There had been no injuries and there was no feeling of urgency to curb their high spirits.

At last, when we pulled into Jim's home station, I looked at my watch. It had taken us five hours and forty-five minutes to cover thirty-five miles—or was it thirty-eight!

The Glen

JIM'S FATHER DIDN'T LOOK AT ALL LIKE the stalwart football type that Jim had described. He was a man of medium height and his shoulders sloped like a pear. His face was stern but his lips drew back into a quick smile when he saw us, though his eyes remained cold and detached. When at last he remembered to remove his long-billed cap I could see that the sandy-white hair only ringed his head. He smiled again, and this time the ice-blue eyes twinkled with devilment. With that smile he won my heart. The greetings over, he beckoned to a tall man loafing against the station shed.

"Come on over, John J. You remember John J., don't ye, Jim? Still lives across the river. Spoke to him to come and meet yez soon's I got the telegram in the mail."

"How've ye been, John J.?" said Jim, holding out his hand.

"Goot! Goot!" nodded John J. "Are them all yer t'ings? Ye ready fer to go now? Best get started. There's no lights on the car."

John J. Campbell stood six feet three inches tall. His hair was red; his eyes a watery blue that contradicted the smile on his lips; and although his face was flabby it could not be called weak. His trousers were held up by a rope which made them ruffle round the waist. The length of his legs explained the ruffle. No standard-sized trousers could accommodate the length of his legs and his waist measurement in the same garment.

John J. opened the door of an old Chevy and motioned to us to get in. Before we had time to take our seats a man, who must have been over seventy, detached himself from a group of men loitering on the platform. Although the day was warm he wore high rubber boots and carried an old yellow raincoat on his arm. A battered felt hat sat on the top of his ears and a wide red handlebar moustache covered his upper lip. The moustache looked so heavy on the thin pallid face that I half expected it to fall off.

"Cummina Hashen!" he called, running towards Jim. "Welcome home!"

"Sean MacLellan! You old so-and-so," said Jim, pumping the limp hand. "You still around?"

"Aye! They can't kill me...."

Mr. Douglas had taken his seat beside the driver and John J. was impatiently accelerating the motor.

"Ye'll be out home before they go, Sean?" said Mr. Douglas. "John J. wants to git goin' now. Don't forget, drop over."

I WASN'T ABLE TO SEE MUCH of the countryside as the glass in the two rear windows had been replaced by corrugated cardboard. The springs in the seat defined the thin upholstery and spiralled up under me until I felt like a Jack-in-the-box. When at last we pulled up at Mr. Douglas' home, Jim leaned over and in his anxiety to get out wrenched the handle off the door. The door fell off its hinges.

"What have I done?" said Jim, his face red with embarrassment. "I pushed hard but not that hard. Wuz it broke?"

"Twuz only stuck in there," said John J., throwing out our bags, "think nothing of it."

Mrs. Douglas, Jim's stepmother, stood at the front door waiting for us.

"Cummina Hashen!" she shouted, grabbed my hand and planted a wet kiss on my cheek. Clemmie Douglas was at least twenty years younger than her husband; her movements were quick and her hair black.

"Cummina Hashen, Jim! How have you been?" she said, pumping Jim's hand with vigour. "I s'pose yez are hungry. Come in...come in...."

"Wait, John J." said Jim, trying to free his hand, "I've a drink somewhere's in this junk...."

"Never mind that now, Jim," said John J., "Molly and me'll be over."

We went into the house. Clemmie herded us all into the big kitchen-dining room.

"Yez can just sit anywhere at all," she said, making sure that her husband secured his proper place at the head of the table.

"Dougall came over and I gave him tea. I ate

too. No tellin' when the train would git here." Clemmie laughed, but there was no warmth in her laughter. "You know Dougall, Jim? He gives Daddy a hand with the chores. He's got his uncle's place, ye know, on the MacTavish Road, but he ain't there much."

The smell of baked beans filled the air as Clemmie placed a large bean crock before us. I was just about to help myself when I noticed that no one else had moved. I looked around the table. Everyone sat with bowed head. I drew back my hand and waited. Mr. Douglas raised his hand and blessed himself. I hastily did the same.

THERE WAS A PARTY OR DANCE every night. Sometimes they were in a neighbour's house and sometimes in a barn. The farm machinery was taken out and long planks laid on logs along the walls as seats for the onlookers. At the far end a small stage was hastily nailed together for the fiddler. He alone occupied this important place, erected perhaps in gratitude and in the hope that he would play till dawn without payment.

I had never been to a dance like this before. Young men danced with old women, and no self-respecting girl would turn down a set with a white-haired old man. Everyone danced for the sheer love of dancing. Dancers of seventy and over got thunderous applause when, after no more than two or three calls, an old man stood up and danced a "solo a'fore" as they called it. No one asked the fiddler for special music. He knew what to play. Old as some of the dancers were, they never missed a step and the watchers laughed and clapped their hands like children. Old Mr. Douglas asked me to dance.

"Oh, no! I couldn't!" I said, finding myself the centre of attention. "I used to dance back home when I was young, but the dances were different."

"Who cares?" shouted Clemmie. "Jim'll dance with me in the same set. Don't worry, we'll see you through." She pushed me to the floor. We danced the set to gales of laughter and no one minded my mistakes.

"It's swell," I said when I found my breath.

When the older folks had had enough of dancing, and the sips the women had taken made them as mellow as the men, the young folk had the dance floor to themselves. The old and the very young went into the house to listen to storytellers. Every man had his own story to tell. Stern faces broke into smiles. Old men seemed to hypnotize the children with their antics.

Then a woman's voice called on Peter to sing. Peter, a lanky man with a bald head, waited until many voices joined in, then he picked up his chair and carried it into the centre of the room. He nodded to his son who struck a chord on his guitar before starting what must have been the longest ballad ever written. It had been a long dirge of about sixty verses, yet no one seemed bored and the applause was sincere.

One by one the guests were urged to perform;

many had brought instruments and played without having to be coaxed.

"Mary!" Clemmie whispered. "Come along with me. Old Bill MacMillan, over there, looks like he's lost his last drink—I'll make ye acquainted."

"Cummina Hashen, Bill!" said Clemmie, shaking the old man by the hand. "See ye've got yer pipes. Ye goin' to give us a little tune tonight? This is Jim's wife from the States, she's never heard the pipes."

"Be glad to," he said, thrusting out a gnarled hand and clutching mine. "Glad to make your acquaintances, Ma'am. Welcome home!" Then gathering up his pipes, he blew two or three times into the bag and tried a few notes. Satisfied, he walked over to a corner, turned his back on the audience, and began to play. The sound in the small room was deafening.

"Did ye smell it?" Clemmie whispered.

"I smelt something, what was it?"

"Th' pipes. Old Bill made th' bag himself out of an old ewe's belly...didn't let her cure long enough."

"What a wonderful old man," I whispered. "Did you hear what he said to me? He said—'Welcome home!'"

NOW THAT JIM HAD LEARNED to manipulate John J.'s car door, the trip into Port Hood was very pleasant. The cardboard box-ends that had replaced the glass had gone with the rain and I found a cushion to cover the loose springs in the seat. Jim sat beside John J. and I sat with Clemmie in the back. The men had business in town and Clemmie and I went visiting.

John J. pulled the old Chevy up to the back door of a spotless house on the edge of town. Clemmie led the way towards the kitchen door and the men said they would call for us later. A big raw-boned woman pushed a kettle over the fire as soon as she saw us and held out a calloused hand in greeting.

"Peggy, I want you to meet Jim's wife," said Clemmie, darting cat-and-mouse glances between us. "Jist up from the States. Mr. MacLellan and Jim was in school together, Mary."

"It's nice meeting you, Mrs. MacLellan," I said truthfully.

"I'm Peggy," she answered. "When you say 'Mrs.' makes me feel ye might be the man fer the rent. Glad to know ye. Sit down, sit down, while I get the tea."

It was obvious that Peggy MacLellan had been expecting us, and it was obvious too that she would have been hurt if we hadn't called. What a tea! There was loaf bread, biscuits, pie, two kinds of cookies and shortbread.

"How d'ye like the Glen?" said Peggy, but before I had time to answer Clemmie spoke for me.

"She says she loves Down East. She thinks there's no place like it, don't ye, Mary? And ye should see her with the cows, and herself knows all about chickens, says her father raises 'em."

"Wonder if she'd be liking it so well after the winter," said Peggy, with a laugh. "As far as I'm concerned, any farm's a bad place. I'd rather live on me hands and knees scrubbin' floors or beggin' me way before I'd go back."

"Peggy was borned back of the church in the Glen," said Clemmie. "I'll show ye the house."

"I FELT LIKE A QUEEN," I said as we drove away, "waited on hand and foot. Is it the same in every house?"

"Pretty much," said Clemmie, puffied up like a courting partridge. "I s'pose ye feel as ye never want to see another piece of bread. That waz a big tea. Seven kinds o' bread, I counted 'em."

John J. turned off the highway and up a narrow road.

"It's really beautiful down here," I said, looking up at the trees arching over the road, "the air even smells different."

"You like down here? Why don't ye make a deal with Dougall?" Clemmie whispered.

"A deal with Dougall?" I whispered in reply. "What for?"

"To buy his place."

"Why do you think he'd sell?"

"What does he want with it? He's never there. It takes money to run a house and the two hundred an' fifty acres that goes with it. If it wasn't fer Daddy he wouldn't have it in the first place. Why not ask him anyway? Jist for fun. Ask him what he'll take for it."

"I always loved the country back home. Do you really think he'll sell? How much do you think he'll want?"

"He'd let it go fer little or nothin'. I'm sure of it. Only cost him seventy-five dollars in the first place. He paid up the taxes."

"SEVENTY-FIVE DOLLARS! For a house and over two hundred acres of land!" I couldn't keep the excitement out of my voice.

"Charlie Lawlor wanted to take it out on taxes hisself fer his oldest boy who was getting married, but Daddy got wind of it and asked Dougall why it waz HE didn't git it—him being next of kin and all. He had first chance, if he paid up the taxes before the sale. Daddy helped Dougall find the money." Clemmie leaned forward and tapped Jim on the shoulder.

"All around here wuz afire, Jim, couple of years back. Started with a spark," said Clemmie, sitting back in her seat, "one little spark from the train, passing on the track. It wuz a windy day, it wasn't no time till the whole Glen looked like she wuz going."

"Any places burnt out?" said Jim.

For a moment Clemmie was silent. I looked at her; she was biting her lip.

"I couldn't say," she said tersely. "John J.'d know. He wuz there."

"Did she burn for long?" said Jim.

"Burnt as far as ye can see fer seven days and nights before the rain came," said Clemmie, as though sure of her ground again. "The heat wuz something fierce close by an' ye could smell the smoke strong, back home.

"Ye hauled water with yer truck, John J., ye can tell it better'n me."

"Yisss!" hissed John J., "me and the boys wuz just after getting back from Sydney, and they didn't want us to go home. Yisss! They wanted water right then and there. But being we was hungry and I had groceries fer Molly on the truck, we went home first."

"Listen to 'im!" Clemmie whispered behind her hand. "Ye should've seen 'em that day. I guess it wuz something fierce. Not one of them with a leg to stand on. John J. had a couple o' bottles on him and cases of beer in the back of the truck. Gitting directions all mixed up about where to go fer water and where to take it...which part of the line, I mean, and him that stubborn they had to drag him out to the truck to go back over to the fire. John J. was the only one with a truck, ye know."

"Used a lot of gas that time," said John J., pushing his old cap back on his head. "So many trips, and ye had to go seven miles...fourteen to a trip, and a barrel was gone in a minute. Had about fifteen men on that bucket line. Yisss! And maybe more...."

"Look, Mary!" said Clemmie, gripping my arm. "John J., stop a minute, will you please?"

John J. brought the Chevy to a standstill at the side of the road. We had reached the top of the ridge and the whole Glen lay before us.

"This is as good a place as any to see where all the neighbours live," said Clemmie, sitting up on the edge of her seat. "Ye can see every farm from here. The last farm we just passed, well, that was where Dougall wuz brought up. His father lived there with old Angus, the coffin maker. He's made seventy-two boxes and he's still smart. Wasn't for old Angus, Dougall and the rest of the family would have starved to death when the old lady died—that would be Dougall's mother. Now, see the river below?" said Clemmie, straining to see between John J.'s and Jim's shoulders. "Down there, on the right, is John J.'s place, ye can just see the roof, and a little past is where old Jennie lives, her old man died last fall. She washes the remains of the women around. See where the bridge crosses the river and the house beside it? Well, that's Ronald the Bridge's old home; nobody's there now. The next place up the road is Daddy's."

The few scattered houses were spread out like shoes on a giant spider. There were seven houses, and of the seven only two were painted, the others were grey and weather-beaten.

"The big house up on the hill, to the left, beyond the fork is old Charlie Lawlor's. He's a slink of a Tory, never get him to vote Liberal," said Clemmie with disgust.

"What a beautiful place!" I said, admiring the

gleaming white house and the neatly hedged fields. "It only goes to show it can be done!"

"It ain't HIM does it!" said Clemmie with a snort of indignation. "It's them twelve kids of his. He puts every one of them in the fields soon's they're big enough to walk."

"But how did he manage when the children were coming and were too little to help?"

"He had poor Margaret out there then. That was before I come."

Clemmie couldn't find a good word to say for a Tory.

"The road keeps on up the hill between them trees," Clemmie went on, "and on the top ye'll find the farm of old William Barnes, on the right. The best built house around, got two brick flues, must be a fireplace in the parlour."

"Yeh!" said Jim interrupting his thoughts, "ye should've seen it when the old man was alive, and it was kept up. Painted white with green trimming...got a big basement. The dining room and the parlour was PLASTERED! I guess the old man intended to plaster all the walls, but the First World War came along...and when he lost his two sons he just gave up...."

"Old Willie got the place from his uncle, ye know," said Clemmie, breaking the silence. "He's rich, got all kinds of money, and he's deaf as a post and queer in the head. Won't buy groceries for himself and that starving dog of his. Keeps the dog out in the winter and the summer; not another living creature on the place. The old dog makes the rounds for handouts every day then goes home and lays there on the doorstep."

"The other road at the fork, where does that go to?" I asked, leaning over Jim's shoulder.

"That's the MacTavish Settlement Road," said Jim. "The big barn just up a piece is Dougall's place, the house is hid beyond the barn. The MacTavish farm is a good three miles up, and beyond, another half mile is the Beatons. Ye can't see them."

"There's five bachelors and one spinster living in them two places," said Clemmie, with a giggle. "Used to be a whole settlement of them. None of the boys would be after taking a prize for beauty except maybe Lauchie MacTavish—when he was young. He was away for years, come home a while back when the old folks died. I guess the boys wrote him they wouldn't take care of Dave—he's the dummy—said they was going away. Course it was only an excuse to git him to keep them all."

"Can see the fire tower," said Jim pensively.

"Where? Show me, Jim?" I said leaning forward.

"Up there, to your right, on the top of the mountain at the head of the Glen. You can just make it out, standing like a pencil against the sky."

"That's a job I wouldn't care about having," said Clemmie, giggling again. There was no mirth in Clemmie's giggles. "Up there, with no one to talk to all summer long. In years gone by there was over sixty families living on that mountain; they built a church and all, but they're all gone now."

"Yes!" said Jim, "I suppose that church must be a hundred and twenty years old and more. All the studding and beams held together by wooden pegs. The boards was hewed by hand and wider than you'd ever see around now. No tree big enough now, all second growth."

"And all painted," said Clemmie, "inside and out. White and pure as the Blessed Virgin herself. There's many a story about that old place."

We sat in silence for a few minutes.

"Ye remember the story of the Protestant girl, Jim?" said Clemmie. Her voice was quieter now. "She ran away from home to be a nun and followed the blaze marks on the trees to git to the coast to catch a ship to Montreal. When it got dark she couldn't see the marks no more and would have been lost for sure if she hadn't come on the little church in the clearing."

"Aye!" said Jim. "I remember. She made herself a bed with spruce boughs and fir on a rock, there in the graveyard. Then made her way to the coast in the morning."

"Aye!" continued Clemmie, "and her Daddy caught up with her there and took her back home. She tried again a couple of years after and they didn't catch up with her that time."

"Couldn't have been any bachelors living up there in them days," hissed John J., "or she'd niver have got by."

Clemmie's loud laughter woke me from my daydream. That night I wrote to my father..."Daddy, I have found Elysium...."

IT WASN'T LATE when I came downstairs the following morning yet I knew that Clemmie had been waiting for me.

"What did Jim say about Dougall's place?" she said without waiting for me to speak. "Did you ask him?"

"Yes, I did," I replied, wishing I didn't have to share my excitement with Clemmie. "Jim didn't want to give in. I wish we had more time, it would have been better if I could have suggested it to him and let him think it over for a few days. Jim's kind of stubborn and likes to think he has thought things out for himself."

"I know just what you mean," said Clemmie pushing a cup of tea across the table to me. "Have to do that meself with Daddy. But did he say 'yes'?"

"He did. But he said that I'd have to do the dickering, he won't have anything to do with that."

"What are ye going to offer him?"

"I don't know. I haven't an idea. What do you think?"

"He'd jump at a hundred...'specially if he'd seen the cash."

I replied, "O.K.... I'll offer him a hundred the first chance I get."

MASS WAS HEARD at the little church in the

Glen on the first Sunday of our visit. The farms were so scattered and the priest had three parishes to serve, so Mass was only heard every other Sunday.

Jim harnessed the mare and brought the buggy round to the door and we all got in. The little mare took her time climbing the hill past Charlie Lawlor's driveway and spruce-hedged fields. From the brow of the hill the land sloped gently down to the church sheltered behind a grove of trees. It was a clear sunny morning and the countryside looked newborn. We passed William Barnes' fine house standing in the centre of fields rank with weeds.

"That's Ronnie and Christina's place," said Clemmie, pointing to a house nearly as large as William Barnes' that stood listless in the morning light. It had never been painted. "Ronnie's family settled the land, ye know, and that's where he took Christina as a bride. She don't help him none. Won't go into the fields or nothing. Ronnie plows, discs and seeds all by hisself. Big place too. Too bad he married that one."

We drove past Ronnie's rich land; many cows and calves grazed contentedly there. When we reached the church Jim tied the mare to the fence that surrounded the graveyard. Then everyone descended on us to bid us welcome and when the priest drove up we all followed him into the church.

The main west door opened into a little vestibule. On the right a flight of stairs led up into the balcony where a wheezy old organ was playing. I dipped my fingers into the Holy Water and followed Clemmie and Mr. Douglas through the swinging doors into the church. In the centre of the nave stood an ancient wood-burning stove, its flue held precariously by wires suspended from the roof. A statue of the Blessed Virgin stood on the left of the altar.

Clemmie nudged me and pointed to a pew next to the altar.

"That used to be old Archie Mac's but he died last month. You and Jim take it."

Little did I know then that this pew would be our own for all time. I wasn't very pious during Mass though the beads dangled through my fingers. I couldn't help thinking about my neighbours.

"For Gawd's sake, Mary, sit still," Jim whispered, "everyone's looking at ye."

When Mass was over I counted fifty adults and God knows how many children. I knew the records of the church must have the names of every member of every family back to the original settlers, and the connections between one family and another, for all would be related, in one degree or another.

I could see that the families living near the church were a little more prosperous than the families living in our Glen. It had been the coming of public utilities that had given them their prosperity. The parish spread over seventy-two miles of farm and wood land. Only the families living near the church had persuaded the power and telephone companies to extend their lines as far as their homes.

"Aye!" said old Mr. Douglas, "everything stops at the church—the power, the telephone, and the snow plow turns at the gate in winter...the gate to the graveyard...."

WHEN WE WERE ALL SETTLED DOWN at the dinner table I had to ask the question that had been plaguing me all morning.

"Jim, I've been thinking about Dougall's place. Any chance of you taking me up to look round after dinner?"

"Are you crazy?" said Jim, putting down his knife and fork, "that's the last thing ye want to do if ye want to git it."

"He'd never sell if he caught ye snooping around," said Clemmie, "that's for sure."

"Best ye stay away," said old Mr. Douglas solemnly, "if yer set on gittin' it. Sure to make Dougall mad, then he'd not sell fer Gawd's sake."

"Seems like we're taking a chance," I said, "buying without seeing the house. I'd like to get an idea what the rooms look like...I'd like to measure the floors and windows...."

"Jim can tell ye that," said Clemmie, "he's been there often enough. It's kind of run down now, but before Dougall's uncle moved out, ye couldn't ask for a better place to go visitin'."

"Aye!" said old Mr. Douglas, stirring his tea, "and a'fore when the old people was living."

"How many were there in the family?" I asked trying desperately to get some idea of the size of the house.

"They had eight kids"—Clemmie giggled—"and the old people before the oldest boy got married; then his wife and kids lived there too; course by then the girls was married and leaving but there was still plenty room left."

"Dougall's father used to be phooey 'bout people traipsin' over his place," said Clemmie, scraping the plates and throwing the scraps to the dog. "Dougall comes by it honest. The old man used to hunt everywhere's he pleased—even in the neighbours' grain fields and them ready for reapin'—but just let anyone go near HIS place! The old 'bodach' had ears like a cat and I swear he stayed awake night and day. I remember one time my eldest brother got wind of the old man hunting on our land and taking our deer without even a 'by yer leave' and then chasing him every time he went by his place with a gun...an' one night he went up to old Dougall's place figgerin' to git a deer he'd seen coming to an old apple tree on the edge of the meadow. It was four in the morning, mind ye, when the deer came in. My brother shot him, dressed him all out an' had started draggin' him to the road, and who came out wavin' his rifle an' yellin' like antiChrist but old Dougall. The slink had been laying there waiting, just waiting till me brother had done all the work. D'you know the old devil took the deer away and told me brother if he ever came back on his place hunting again it would be his last time."

"Aye!" said Mr. Douglas, nodding his head, "if ye want that place it's best ye stay away."

Clemmie finished clearing the table in silence. Jim pushed back his chair and walked over to the window and stood there looking out over the field. "What ever happened to Willie MacSween?"

Clemmie threw her wet dishcloth down on the table so hard that it sounded like the crack of a rifle.

"Willie MacSween?" she said. "He's dead an' wandering."

"Died in the fire." Mr. Douglas' voice was very quiet and it seemed difficult for him to say the words. "Him and Martha, no one knows exactly. He went by Sean's yellin' 'fire' and Sean and his brother Frank took off across the river. John J. found Willie after, or what was left of him and the mare...harness rings and the wheels. Looked like he was in the wagon heading out. Martha wasn't with him. John J. found her halfway to his place. Willie must've left without her. Maybe she took too long gitting started...."

"Maybe she did," said Clemmie, "God rest her soul."

IT WAS MAIL DAY. Clemmie started shining up the house early in the morning. The neighbours came early and stayed to gossip. After greeting each person Clemmie expertly stripped each one of what news they had, but it was different with Christina, a tall, thin, black-haired woman. As soon as she arrived Clemmie whipped the coat off her shoulders and led her over to the settee. In a flash Christina had a cup of tea in her hand and Clemmie one in hers and the two sat huddled together, whispering. At last, when the cups had been returned to their saucers for the last time I saw Clemmie run her tongue swiftly over her lips like a cat after a dinner of goldfish. She followed Christina to the door and without drawing breath continued—"Christina says that Anne Margaret, over at MacLaughlins', is going to have a baby—she's one o' them at the Home in Sydney, ye know. She says it's been somethin' awful to see all the young fellers hangin' around there. She's the one to be tellin', the slink! After all she done to poor Ronnie."

"Christina makes me feel nervous," I said, "those black eyes of hers seem to see through my skin and I begin to feel that my face is dirty."

Clemmie didn't have time to reply for the door opened and Dougall ambled into the kitchen, sat down on the settee and began rolling a cigarette.

"Himself says we'd let the hay go till next week and I thought I'd get the boys at John J.'s to mow me place tomorrow. Git her in in half a day easy, place is run down so bad it's only short."

I caught Clemmie's eye and she signalled me to speak up.

"Dougall!" I said, hoping my voice was steady. "Would you think of selling your place?"

"Why? Ye thinking of buyin' her?" Dougall's eyes never left the cigarette he was rolling.

"Well, I thought it might be nice to live here. Would you sell?"

"Weeel nooow!" Dougall drawled cagily, "I just don't know that I want to sell."

"I'll give you a hundred dollars CASH!" I said quickly.

"Wouldn't sell for no hundred, if I WAS gonna sell."

"How about a hundred and fifty?" I said, trying to keep him from stalling. "Jim said that's as high as I can go."

"Weeel nooow, ye see, it ain't the money so much...exactly. I might as well tell ye...I might be after gitting married meself one o' them days and I'll want the house meself."

"That's different," I replied, trying to hide my disappointment, "if you're getting married...."

"MARRIED! YOU gittin' married?" screamed Clemmie, "and who is it ye'll be marryin'?"

"Well, I ain't asked 'er exactly...just yet, but I was thinking of asking Olive."

"OLIVE!" Clemmie couldn't believe her ears. "Ye haven't wrote her, have you?"

"No!" said Dougall, pausing to light the cigarette dropping from his lips, "but I'm thinking about it."

"Where is Olive?" I asked impatiently. "Could you write and get an answer back in a week? We have to go back to New York next week."

"Weeel, all right then! I'll git a letter away t'night." And with that Dougall got up and went outside to join the men.

"Olive!" said Clemmie, as soon as we were alone. "Where did he pull that one out of? Must've been in that tobacco. He never went out with her in his life. She wouldn't even look at him before she went away, and he thinks she'll marry him? Thinks she'll be ripe for plucking, I s'pose, after being in the Unwed Mothers Home. Three days old now... Ronnie and Christina are gonna take it."

A week went by. Two mail days passed and no letter came from Olive.

OUR VACATION WAS OVER. Tomorrow we would be travelling back to New York and still Dougall refused to make a decision.

"Have the cash handy," Clemmie advised. "He'll likely stall around, but if ye show him the money he'll take it, ye'll see."

The next time Dougall came into the kitchen I didn't waste any time.

"Well, are you going to let us buy your place?"

"Weeel noow! I just can't say. P'raps I'd best wait till herself comes home, then I can talk to her."

I reached for my purse and held out a fifty-dollar bill and five twenties under Dougall's nose.

"Here it is, Dougall, all brand new American money. One hundred and fifty dollars, and you can get the benefit of the exchange. It's your last chance."

Dougall's little eyes followed the bills like a cat watching a fledgling bird.

"Weeel nooow! It would have to be without the hay. Ye'd have to leave the hay for me...being I put her in...or there ain't no deal."

"All right, you can take the hay. Is it a deal then?"

"Could be naaw, could be!" Dougall turned to Clemmie. "Ronnie says Olive is coming home next week. No need for no rush. I'll have to talk to her." Dougall quickly left the kitchen.

That night there was a little gathering at the house in our honour. Before dawn it had turned into a regular party. Jim and I were to leave on the afternoon train but we couldn't make it. John J. hadn't arrived with the car. Late that afternoon Jim went over the river and between him and John J. they decided it would be best to get the night train from Port Hawkesbury.

The rain had become a deluge by the time John J. drove up in his truck. The back was now covered with tarpaulin like a prairie schooner. Sitting on the seats hastily constructed with stumps and cross-boards were Dougall and four men.

"These fellas want to get to the vendor," said John J., oblivious of the mud he was tracking into the kitchen, "and I'm dry meself. Maybe Jim, if ye and the Missus be ready, maybe we could go now.... If we hurry we'll catch the vendor."

"What on earth would we be doing in Port Hawkesbury all that time between six o'clock and the train time?" said Jim indignantly.

"Molly's got people there, we'll find something to do. Andy MacTavish has his fiddle with him in the back."

"Jim, ye'd best go," said Clemmie, drawing Jim into the pantry, "John J.'s not the most responsible man in the world, and if ye let him get away on ye, he might not come back for a week."

We got into Port Hawkesbury as the manager of the liquor store reached up to pull down the blinds. The door was still opened and every man went in. Jim went in with the rest of them. In a few minutes he came running out and threw open the door.

"If ye want Dougall's place ye'd best give me the money. He'll sell!"

We drove over to the railway station and parked in the yard. It was too late to get the deed of sale drawn up but that could be sent by mail for Jim's signature. No one was around and it was raining so hard that we were not afraid of getting caught by the Mounties. Jim, John J. and I crawled into the back of the truck with the others. Andy played his heart out and Dougall got up and danced a solo.

When the train came in I helped Jim into the car, found the tickets in his pocket and handed them to the conductor. Jim never heard the farewell tune Andy played for us on the station platform in the rain...he was fast asleep.

Our New Home

WE HAD SCUTTLED OUR SKIFFS! We were back in the Glen with all our worldly possessions covered with a tarpaulin on the back of a shiny new truck. We no longer had our apartment or our jobs in New York City. The Glen was our home. I couldn't help feeling frightened when I realized what we had done. We had driven through teeming rain for hundreds of miles, but this morning the truant sun broke through the clouds and the air was sweet and warm. After dinner we sat outside and talked. Jim was tired and wouldn't say very much even to his father.

"We got the wire with the money ye sent," said Mr. Douglas, as he stopped to pick up a whittling twig at his feet. "And we fenced the bottom field. We had to make a bush fence along the river. Too much brush to clear for wire fencing. Can't see her from the road nohow."

"Good!" said Jim, livening up a little. "How much do I owe you and the boys?"

"Yez'll stay here a while. The house ain't fit," said Clemmie, drying her hands on her apron.

"Sandy ain't doing nothing right now," said Mr. Douglas, holding his whittling twig at arm's length so his far-sighted old eyes could see better. "I suppose he's about the only one ain't busy...he'd be too, if it wasn't for he's after getting shaky. His work beats most o' them around here. It's just that he's getting slow."

"Well, we'd best see what needs doing," said Jim stretching his legs. "Get an idea where to start. How about it Dad? Feel like taking a walk?"

"Let's all go," I said jumping up. "I'm longing to see inside the house. It's been terrible having to wait so long."

We walked up the narrow road cut through the forest for about half a mile. The grass between the wagon tracks was still damp from the rain and cool to walk on. The tall spruce sheltered us from the heat of the sun until we reached the boundary of our property. Now I could see the wire and the freshly peeled fence posts gleaming in the sunlight. I looked up at Jim, hoping to see that he was sharing my happiness, but his face was stern. He was looking down at the soil. I noticed then how thin the grass was. Even the daisies were scrawny. They barely had enough strength to keep their heads up.

"Might as well plow the works," said Jim. I felt he was talking to himself rather than to me. I slipped my arm through his.

Our house and barn stood on a rise above the road, and our small fields were the only cleared lands to be seen on this side of the river. On the far side I could see John J.'s pasture cut like a giant swathe through the trees. We turned up a grass-grown track dividing our fields above the road. We couldn't see our house until we passed the gaunt unpainted barn. It was a small low house, with one window on either side of the front door, and an extension tacked onto one end like a pan handle. The builders had neglected to include a window or adequate supports for the roof, which sagged like a sway-backed horse.

"They must have had a frolic to put up that house, and everyone must have been cockeyed by the time they reached the windows." My remark was greeted with silence. No one else saw anything funny in those two front windows tilting towards the door like a deaf man straining to hear. I ran up to the door and waited for Jim to unlock it.

"What are ye waiting for?" said Clemmie, "it's not locked. Nobody around here locks doors. Ye'd never know who'd come by needing shelter."

Jim stepped up beside me, turned the knob, and pushed open the door. We walked inside and found ourselves in the front room. There was no porch or hall. The room was empty, the floor covered in dust, but I could see that the boards were wide and worn thin with constant scrubbing with hard soap. The knots stood out like warts on a toad's back. A pile of bricks lay on the floor where a fireplace had once stood. In the rear wall, facing the window, were two doors no more than three feet apart.

"This was the guest room in days gone by,"

said Clemmie, opening one of the doors. "Many's the one slept here."

There were three articles in the little cell-like room: a small nail keg, the rim and sides stained with yellow scum, a rickety old rocking chair, and a filthy blanket thrown over it. I turned to the second door.

"I want ye to see the kitchen," said Clemmie, blocking my way. "We'll see that room after."

As soon as I stepped into the kitchen I could understand Clemmie's enthusiasm. It was a bright sunny room with two windows, one opening on the front of the house and the other facing west to the sway-backed shed. The floor boards groaned and sagged under our weight and there was a gaping hole under the front window where rain had seeped through the twisted frame and rotted the boards. In the centre of the room a wood-burning stove stood on three legs, covered in rust and surrounded by bricks from a fallen flue. The only furniture was a small table and a chair that had lost its rungs and stood as uncertainly as a new-born calf. There were no water taps, no sink, not even a pump.

"Have to get water down below," said Clemmie, reading my thoughts. "Tis a good well though. Never goes dry winter or summer."

"She means a spring," said Jim, knowing I wouldn't understand. "I remember it. Water cold as ice all summer long." Jim turned to his father. "Is she dug out?"

Clemmie didn't give his father time to answer. "Oh yes! We've been pasturing our cows up here. Daddy kept her open for to water them."

"Is this the pantry?" I asked, pointing to a door at the back of the room.

"No!" said Clemmie, breathing down my neck. "That was the old folks' bedroom."

It would take more than a name to give that narrow little room the dignity of being called a bedroom. I did not dare cross the threshold. The floor sagged in the centre and in places had rotted completely away. Through the window I could see a tumble-down shed surrounded by weeds and rusty farm machinery.

"This will have to be the pantry," I said firmly. "The carpenter can build shelves along the wall and a bench and cupboards below. There'll be just enough room left to work in. I'll have to have a pantry." I closed the door quickly and nearly tripped over an iron ring set in a loose square of flooring just behind me.

"That's the cellar, such as it is," said Mr. Douglas, holding out his arm to steady me. "Best take a look, Jim."

Jim bent down, grasped the ring and lifted the trap.

A dank mouldy smell seeped into the kitchen. In the murky light I saw a ladder leading down into the darkness below. Jim replaced the trap quickly.

"What's upstairs?" said Jim looking around. "Where ARE the stairs?"

"Back there, some place," said Mr. Douglas,

leading the way into a room beside the old folks' bedroom.

"This was the dining room," said Clemmie, "and that door beyond goes into the front room."

"It's no bigger than the pantry," I said, deciding not to worry about what Clemmie would think.

"Here's the stairs," said Jim, pointing to a ladder in the corner that led up to a trap in the ceiling.

"And that was the pantry," said Clemmie, her face twisted into a smile. She pointed to three narrow shelves under the ladder laden with three chipped soup bowls and an ancient condiment set.

"How in heaven did they manage? You said there were eight children, and the old folks?"

"Yeh! And they was lucky to have it!"

"Come on!" said Jim, climbing the ladder, "let's see what's upstairs. I'll soon get some light down." Jim pushed up the trap and let it rest on the floor above. Mr. Douglas and Clemmie followed. I reached the top step and looked over. A flimsy partition of boards divided off a large room over the kitchen from the rest of the attic. Rafters, braces and studs stood uncovered. The only door, without knob or catch, sagged on its only hinge. Lacy cobwebs hung from the rafters to within inches of the floor and filtered the sunlight pouring in through a window in the western gable. The only furniture was an old iron bedstead with hammock springs. It had been painted many times with different colours, but it was hard to tell which colour had last been applied. The mattress was made up of bags of oat straw placed three abreast over the springs, and ancient straw dropped from jagged holes in the burlap. Then one of the rags moved, and from deep inside I heard squeaking.... Rats! I fled down the ladder. Clemmie wasn't far behind me.

"Take the whole shootin' match outside, Jim," I heard Mr. Douglas say. "Make one big fire, bag and all. It's the only thing."

I reached the kitchen safely, but a huge rat, at least a foot long, ran across the floor right in front of me. I screamed and ran out into the yard.

Jim and Mr. Douglas got rid of the rats. They could carry only one bag at a time down the ladder. The burlap was so rotten that it required both hands to hold it together. I was terrified that something more than straw would fall out of those bags. Then the men went down to the barn and came back with shovels. Jim struck a match and started the fire. Fanned by a light breeze the flames roared upward. Then the squeaking began. I covered my ears and turned away. I didn't uncover them until Mr. Douglas and Jim had stopped circling the burning heap and the flames had died down. Not a single rat escaped.

So this was to be my home. A house occupied by insects and rats. A house in need of a roof, floors, and a chimney. A structure without a single straight wall or window, and in need of gallons of paint. But it was our own. Our only home. It was beautiful!

THE FOLLOWING DAY was Sunday, and the Sunday for Mass. It was useless asking old Sandy to start work until the following Monday. As it was, it took Jim most of Sunday evening to coax and wheedle the old man to work at all. It was only after Jim promised to drive him to and from work that he agreed. The arrangement suited us very well. We couldn't let the old man sleep in the house the way it was. Goodness knows when the old range would be delivered, and the nights were cold.

Old Sandy was a man in his fifties. His head was thatched with sparse sandy hair. His chin and neck sprouted bristles in abundance, which lay like mown hay on his transparent skin. The apex of Sandy's head was not his bald pate but the tip of his Roman nose. The rest of his head receded from that point and gave him the appearance of a large mouse. His head wobbled up and down without ceasing.

It was a hot day, but old Sandy wore a flannel shirt of faded green plaid, buttoned up to the neck. His hands, small and finely moulded, shook in all directions as he grasped a board and laid it across an improvised bench. He picked up the saw and held it poised and quivering in the air. I waited breathlessly for his next move. It came suddenly. The saw plunged unerringly and swift as a hawk on its prey. With one movement, a deep cut was made. Sandy did not stop until the ends fell apart. He held the ends up for inspection, and with a grunt and many nods of the head, measured the smaller piece with his rule. When he came to rebuild the flue, there was the breathless moment before the mortar or the brick came down into exact place.

Old Sandy shook his way through room after room. He repaired the floors, straightened the windows, tore down the wall between the dining room and the little guest room. Slowly and meticulously he made a hallway and stairs that I could use with comfort. He made me a pantry with cupboards and shelves, and hung sheets of plaster board to cover the walls.

Now that the rats had gone and the new staircase was built, I could explore the rest of the attic. Through the cobweb curtains I found a butter tub made by Jim's grandfather, who was a cooper and had never been known to use a nail, and parts of a spinning wheel. The tub was a little pile of staves surrounded by two hoops. Jim picked it up.

"I'll take it down and put it together," he said. "Be just as good as ever when I soak it in water."

We found from the beginning that water would be a problem. The spring down in the field was pure, but the incline was steep. And after a few trips with brimming buckets, we decided that for washing and cleaning we would depend on a natural basin in the ground near the house that gathered and collected surface water. We bought galvanized buckets and set up a washstand on a homemade bench in the kitchen. One bucket was designated drinking water, the other cleaning. We had plenty of money when we chose our range, but no idea how little it would prove to be before we had established our home. With hopes in the sky I decided against a stove with a reservoir for hot water. I had planned on a large tank attached to a waterfront in the stove. Now I found myself with no way of heating water but the tea kettle, until I found, on one of the back pages in a catalogue, a five-gallon blue enamel pot suitable for canning. I sent for it immediately.

It was Clemmie who suggested we ask Sean, the water diviner, to find a place for us to sink a well. Neither of us thought to ask whether Sean had ever found water. And at the time, it didn't seem strange to find Sean was free or that, with a water diviner in the community, everyone lugged pails of water up steep hills and over long distances.

The first day Sean showed up for work, he came into the kitchen for a cup of tea and a smoke. A strange man! His ghostly white skin was startling enough, so thin that the veins showed through like cobwebs on a ceiling. Clemmie had told me that Sean wore every stitch of clothing he owned, winter and summer. It was nothing, she said, to find underneath his flannel shirt another flannel shirt, and under that still another. On his feet, high black gum-shoes, a full size large to accommodate all his socks, were kept tightly laced against the snow in winter, and for no reason at all in summer. It was joked—"Sean washed his feet t'other day and found a pair of socks been lost since a year."

His tea finished, Sean took his tools out of the gunnysack he carried over his shoulder and unwrapped each drill from its individual wrapper and spread them out in the sun to glisten. He then covered them with the gunnysack and came back into the kitchen for another cup of tea before going home for supper.

Sean was back before breakfast the next morning. He pulled a forked alder from some place under his coveralls and explained at great length the infallibility of his "machine" when he wished to find water near the surface. Jim, of course, had work to do outside, but I was delayed a full hour from my work while I learned the great mystery.

Sean, with his alder firmly grasped in both hands, forked prongs pointing down, walked all around the house. I peeked out now and then from one window or another. Sean was always there, no matter which window I stood beside. He came in for dinner.

"Found a place just outside the porch door," he said, indicating the door to the sway-backed shed. "Fork jumped near out of my hand. Start drillin' tomorrow." I watched him go.

Just in time for dinner, three days later, I saw Sean coming round the barn. I put out another plate. Sean and Jim came into the kitchen together.

"Where was ye?" said Jim. "What happened?"

Sean grinned and took off his coat.

"Was ye longing?" was all he said.

Not a sod had been turned when Sean came in later looking for his tea.

"Well, the drills be all rigged up. Start the drilling now," he said, when he finished his tea.

I heard sounds of shipping shortly afterwards. Sean worked until suppertime.

After supper he went home, and Jim called me out to see what he had done. Sean had been lucky. He had been drilling in sand, and his drill was down four feet.

"Do you think we'll ever be able to pump water out of that little hole?" I asked. Jim shrugged his shoulders and covered the drill.

Sean didn't come back for eight days. But on the ninth, he came just after sun-up. At ten o'clock he found an excuse to go home.

"Run into rock," he said. "Me drills are all dull, have to get them sharpened. Be back tomorrow."

By now there was a little path circling a hole two feet in diameter. Jim measured the depth. Sean had gained another two feet. This time neither of us spoke, but Jim was not so careful about covering the drills and leaving them exactly as he found them.

A month later Sean showed up again. Then, to justify his appearance, he went out and began drilling. It wasn't long before he was back in for his tea. He talked and talked until I served supper, and only stopped talking long enough to swallow his food. At last, in desperation, Jim offered to drive him home.

"Ye're welcome to stay if we had the other bed up," said Jim, a little ashamed of himself. "But we only have the floor to offer. I'll take ye home in the truck, if ye'd rather."

"Might as well," said Sean, draining his glass. "There's nothing to be done till ye dig where the cave-in is."

This was the first we had heard of any cave-in.

"Yisss!" Sean went on, "she caved *in to*day. Couldn't get the drill down at the last of it. Ye dig down and open her up, and I'll be back when ye're finished."

That was the story of the hole outside the door to the sway-backed shed. Sean never did come back. His drills lay out under the snow all winter.

GETTING STOCK FOR THE FARM was no problem. Everyone had a cow or a calf for sale, or had a friend who was looking for a buyer. We bought an old cow named Star. She was a good milker. Jim knew how to milk, but we had made a deal that I would milk if he built the morning fires. I had to learn, and old Star gave two full gallons of milk twice a day—and two five-pound lard pails as well.

Clemmie had a ten-month-old bull calf that she offered as company for the cow. I soon discovered that all bull calves were left with full potency until they were butchered!

"Mary, I s'pose ye're like the others around here. Foolish over calves," said Mr. Douglas, who walked up the road to see how we were getting along. "Feller over to the church ships cream. Gets rid of his calves. P'haps he got one now. If he hasn't, there's others over there shipping too."

At my urging Jim took his father to the church and brought back a pair of week-old calves.

"They're broke to drink from a bucket, no trouble," said the old man. I felt he was proud to have done his part in helping us stock our farm.

"I don't know how we'll feed them come this winter," said Jim. "And we'll have to get a horse."

"Ye'll get a few ton of wild hay off the place," said Mr. Douglas. "Not much good, but better'n nothin'. And John J. has hay for sale most years."

Mr. Douglas made a special trip to tell us about Silver. His owner had three horses, and because the other two worked as a team, Silver had to go. She was a lovely haughty grey mare and looked more like a quarter horse than a farm drag. Everyone offered us cats to keep down the rats, and Clemmie's old dog had pups....

I ordered day-old chickens from a hatchery in Truro, with instructions that they were to be sent to the station for collection. Jim was fencing the day they were to arrive, so I took the truck and stopped to pick up Mr. Douglas to save him going to pick up the mail in the buggy. The train had just left when we arrived at the station. There was no sign of a box of chickens.

"You're sure?" I asked the station manager. "A notice came in the mail telling me the chicks would arrive today."

"Nothing come off the train but what you seen here," he said pointing to the three skimpy mail bags Mr. Douglas had picked up. "Come to think of it though, Ben, the wagon man did have chickens in the car...I heard 'em yeepin'."

I ran to the truck, started up the motor, and turned down the road to town.

"Hi! Where do ye think ye're goin'?" said Mr. Douglas, grabbing his hat.

"The chickens are on the train!"

"Foolishness!" the old man grumbled and braced himself for the bumpy road. He hung on to his hat, pushed his feet against the floorboards, and glared at the road.

"Nope!" said the station manager, at the next stop. "No chickens here."

"I'll have to catch them," I cried, "the nights are cold. They'll die in a station with no heat if they're left overnight."

"Might be ye could catch the train. She's only 'bout five minutes ahead of ye."

I took the right turn into the main road. Incredulity, followed by amazement and finally anger, swept over Mr. Douglas' face. He was speechless. He bumped, clutched, and braced himself all the way to the next station. The chicks were still on the train, and the train still five minutes ahead of us. There was nothing I could do but drive on to the end of the line—seventeen miles away. The old man didn't say a word.

The chicks were at Caithness station, and the

station manager was very happy to deliver them. On the way home Mr. Douglas never stopped talking.

"I s'pose ye know them chicks might be after costing me me job."

"How, Dad?" I asked, unaware of the depth of his anger.

"What's the bondsman goin' to think? Me chasin' all over the county with Government mail. Like as not they'll pull their names off me bond. And it'd be no more than right."

"Who's going to do that, Dad?"

"Everyone. Like as not, it's all over th' county by now."

"Oh! Come now. It's not as bad as that. They won't be mad when they hear that the chicks would have probably died by morning."

"The postmistress...all three of them will be having fits. All them people sittin' round their kitchen at mealtime waitin' for their mail." The old man was more relaxed now, and his voice was gentle.

"I'll take the blame," I said. I stepped on the accelerator.

"Whoa there! Take it easy! We're better late than going on another ride...the last, maybe!"

The Children

It was mail day. Clemmie Douglas was busy sorting.

"Git yerself a cup o' tea, Mary," she said. "I'll soon be done. And bring one fer me." She picked up a letter and looked at it for a long while before putting it between her teeth. Then she went on with her sorting. When she had finished, she sat down and tore open the envelope.

"Mary, read this!" she said. "It came in the mail."

Mary read the note quickly and felt tears springing to her eyes. Then she read it again, more slowly, until the hot sensation in her throat subsided. She lifted a perfectly composed face to Clemmie. "Are you going to take her?" she asked.

"I can't," Clemmie answered. "Joe'd have a fit. He ain't got the patience no more. Gittin' too old to have little ones around. But I thought maybe you and Jim...."

"Poor, poor, little girl! It would be wonderful. What's she like?" Mary was eager for children.

"She's a little over three, maybe four. Red hair. Blue eyes, round as dollars! Fat, and laughs all the time. Nobody'd ever be sorry for takin' that one."

"I know! I know! I'm sure Jim will say yes. How come she's that old and nobody took her?"

"Her mother took a pain and died one night. Left a whole bunch of kids. Some went to the Home, but the Gillis family took this one. Now Mrs. Gillis is sick herself and can't have the care of her. If ye should want, ye can get the papers, ye know."

LITTLE ANNE FITTED into the lives of Jim and Mary Douglas as if she'd been born to them. They were playing on the floor with her one evening before bedtime, when Jim became suddenly serious.

"She could have a wonderful time with a little brother."

"Oh, Jim! Wouldn't it be nice to give a little boy a home. The way it is, we aren't using up half our hearts."

"When ye married me," Jim teased, "ye promised I was to have all yer heart."

Mary wrapped her arms around her husband and kissed him. Jim blushed, as he always did when she made a display of affection. Ten years of marriage had not altered his essential reticence.

"A little boy," he laughed, untwining the fingers laced around his neck. "A son. Be nice if we could get him b'fore Christmas."

"I don't know, Jim." Mary was serious now. "Maybe the Home wouldn't even have a little boy for adoption that soon. Of course, he'd have to be for adoption. I couldn't bear to give him back—I just couldn't do that."

"No," said Jim gently. "He'd have to be really ours. We'll manage. Maybe we should ask Clemmie about it?"

"Oh, no! I'd just as lief not ask Clemmie," said Mary. "I think maybe sometime Clemmie would like to take children for herself, but she says your father'd not have the patience to put up with them. Anyway, she'd always be thinkin' she had a right to be tellin' us how to raise him. We'll go to the priest. We'll have a thanksgiving Mass said for Anne. That'll give us an opening."

Jim nodded his assent.

On Sunday, after Mass, Jim picked up Anne and walked with Mary to the altar rail, where the three knelt to say a prayer. Then Jim carried Anne over to the creche in front of St. Joseph's shrine. He held her close to the spruce boughs so that she could look into the tiny stable and see the animals, the shepherds, Mary and Joseph, and the Infant Jesus lying in the manger. After a few moments, they found the courage to go into the vestry, where Father Phil was removing his vestments.

"You're new in the parish, aren't you?" he said, extending a hand to Mary, though he knew very well who she was.

"Mary Douglas," she answered hurriedly. "And this is my husband Jim."

"You're Joe Douglas' boy." The priest's voice was comfortably familiar. "I know your people. Good to have you home again."

Jim said it was good to be back and shook the

priest's hand, but was too uncomfortable himself to say any more.

"Thank you, Father." Mary was a little breathless. "We're going to be in the parish from now on, so you'll be seeing a lot of us. This is our little Anne. Her mother died last year. We got her through Jim's people. That's what we came to see you about. We just love her. We're so happy God gave her to us. We'd like you to say a thanksgiving Mass for us." Mary took out the five-dollar bill that was folded in her pocket and offered it to the priest. The usual Mass offering was two dollars, but she wanted to give the appearance of prosperity before making her request.

Father Phil took the folded bill and slipped it into his pocket without once looking at it.

"Is she all that nice?" he smiled, putting a finger under Anne's chin, but looking at Jim. "She brings you that much happiness?"

"Yes, Father." Jim had recovered his composure. "She fills our days. And while you're at it, Father, could you slip in a few words about—maybe—a little brother fer her. Mary and me thought perhaps...fer Christmas?"

"Of course, of course!" said Father Phil, as if their request was the most ordinary thing in the world. "I'm a good friend of the sister in charge of infants at the Home. I'll get in touch with her this week."

Father Phil smiled approvingly on the couple.

The Douglases felt their hearts lift with relief.

There was hope!

Word came the very next mail day. Mary's hands shook a little as she opened the envelope, which contained a short note and a picture of a solemn-faced little fellow. The note read: "We are enclosing a picture of a little boy we have here who is available for adoption. He was left in my charge. He is a very bright little lad, perfect for any home. If you find him satisfactory, you can arrange to call for him on Tuesday, the 12th. We can take care of the papers here, as he has not yet been turned over to the Welfare Services." The note was signed: Sister Frances Theresa.

"TUESDAY!" Mary's mind raced. "That's tomorrow! We'll have to tell Jim's father and Clemmie." Mary knew that any letter with a Sydney postmark left Clemmie bursting with curiosity, but one to her stepson's family simply had to be explained.

"AIN'T THAT THE LITTLE DARLING!" exclaimed Clemmie, when Mary showed her the picture. "Who is he?"

"We're getting a little brother for Anne," Mary blurted. "It's his picture."

Jim's father looked at the picture without comment and passed it back. His eyes had a fixed stare, and his lips were drawn into a thin line. Jim squirmed in his chair, shuffled his feet, and looked to Mary for help. She could think of nothing to say. She was helpless before this stern silent man. She shook her head and stared at her feet. She and Jim had told no one of their plans or problems. She knew how hard it was for Jim to explain himself.

"Dad," Jim's voice was reticent, cautious. "We have to go to Sydney tomorrow to get the boy. Ye'd best take the day off and come along. Do ye good."

The old man's face softened instantly. The awkward moment was over. Jim felt the change and was glad of it, but now he had a problem with Clemmie.

"It'd be nice if you could come too," he said, looking at his stepmother. "But the truck'll only ride three in the seat, and with four, the Mounties'd sure as hell pick us up on the highway. And we have to take Anne along." Jim's voice trailed off.

"That's all right! I couldn't go anyway. Mrs. Lawlor'll be coming down to help me set the cheese." Clemmie was vexed and her words were very clear and a little clipped.

The next morning, at about eight, Jim and Mary drove down to pick up the old man. He was ready and waiting.

"Look, Jim," he whispered. "I've got a little of that—stuff—out back. D'ye think 'twould be safe to take 'er along?"

"Oh, I think so," said Jim, without thinking.

The old man sauntered around to the outhouse and came back with a bulge in his pocket. But he was still not completely confident.

"Yer sure, now? I wouldn't take 'er if ye thought there was any chance of us gettin' caught.

Ye could lose yer license, y'know. Maybe even the truck." He peered earnestly at Jim through his heavy grey eyebrows. "Yer sure, now, it's all right?"

"I still got my U.S. license plates," Jim said. "And everybody says the Mounties don't bother cars with foreign plates much. I don't think we got any real worries."

The old man climbed into the truck. They waved to Clemmie standing in the doorway, and were on their way.

"Perhaps we'd best have a taste before we get to the highway," the old man said. He pulled the package out of his pocket and unfolded the newspaper he'd wrapped the bottle in. Jim took a swig, and Joe Douglas took a longer one. Then he replaced the cork, rewrapped the bottle, and returned the package to his pocket. He felt happy, free but guilty, like a boy playing hooky from school.

"Why don't we take the short cut?" he suggested cheerily. "We'll cut off twenty mile if we go as the crow flies, and the road is not bad at all. Bumpy. But yer truck'll handle 'er easy. Less chance o' runnin' inta the Mounties."

The road was so twisty and bumpy that Mary had a hard time keeping little Anne balanced on her knee. They all got a little giddy as they counted the number of times their heads hit the roof or nearly did. It was after a particularly bad bump that Mary caught the smell of liquor. At first she thought it was only the men's breath in the stuffy cab, but when she shifted Anne to her other knee, the one nearest Jim, the smell became overpowering.

"Do you smell anything?" she asked, glancing at the men.

"Smell anything?" asked Jim. "Like what?"

"Like something a Mountie might like to investigate if he opened the cab door."

"MOONSHINE!" Both men yelled at once.

Jim took his foot off the gas pedal. "Oh, fer God's sake, Dad! Are ye sure ye got the cork in that bottle tight?"

"I banged 'er in with the butt o' me hand. Ye seen me do it, Jim," the old man said, shifting backwards in his seat to raise his buttocks and reach the bottle.

"STOP!" he roared suddenly. "STOP! I'm soaked!"

In his hand, still wrapped in the newspaper that now dripped like a wet blanket, was the bottle of moonshine. He tore off the paper. "My God, Jim! The road must've bumped 'er loose. No more'n one drink apiece. We'd best finish 'er right here. The smell's strong. No tellin' what might happen once we git t'the ferry."

He opened the window, threw out the newspaper, and passed the bottle to Jim.

"Please, Jim," said Mary. "If Sister Frances Theresa smells liquor on your breath, she might think we're not fit parents."

"If she gits one smell of me, that'll fix it." The old man chuckled as he explored his trousers. Then he finished off the rest of the bottle.

THE CHILDREN

"It'll evaporate before we get there," said Mary. "And if it doesn't, you can stay in the truck."

They arrived at the orphanage just before noon. Mary was still concerned about the impression they would make, but she was also eager to make Jim's father feel comfortable in her company and not to have him worrying about the accident.

"Are you coming in, Dad?" she asked anxiously.

"No," he said. "It's best I stay here and dry off a little more. I smell like a distillery. I'd only be causin' ye trouble."

Mary was pleased to hear the cheerful note in his voice. Relieved, she arranged her own dress and little Anne's hair. Then she gave the child to Jim, and the three of them walked up the steps to the Home.

Sister Frances Theresa greeted them warmly and looked over Mary's shoulder.

"Who's that in the truck?" she asked.

"Oh," Mary hesitated. "That's Mr. Douglas...Jim's father." She looked to her husband for assistance and added, "He said he'd rather wait in the truck till we're through."

"Come on in!" Sister called out to him, but the old man merely shook his head.

Reaching around to catch the end of her veil so that it wouldn't blow up around her head, Sister Frances ran out the door and was at the cab of the truck before either Mary or Jim could stop her. She opened the door. Jim looked sick.

"Come in! Come in! Don't be shy," she coaxed. "Nobody's going to sit outside here. The girls have made little cakes, and they have a nice lunch ready for you all. Come on, now, Mr. Douglas. It's not right to disappoint them."

Nobody could resist Sister Frances Theresa.

During the lunch, Mary was uneasy, and Jim nearly dropped his plate. The old man kept his eyes constantly on Sister Frances, and tried to stay as still as a mouse. Once his cup tipped and its hot contents spilled over his trousers. Mary saw him wince and clutch his groin, but Sister seemed to notice nothing. She kept up a friendly chatter, pausing now and then to urge more tea and cakes on her guests, or to entice little Anne to try a soft drink. At last she got up.

"Well, now," she said. "I suppose you're anxious to see your new little boy. You finish your tea, and I'll get him."

When the door closed behind her, Jim let out a long ragged sigh and passed his hand across his forehead. The old man subsided into his chair, and Mary's knotted hands relaxed in her lap. They had been wondering if the delay in producing the child had any meaning, and had shared a silent concern about the clinging aroma of moonshine.

When Sister reappeared with Sonny laughing in her arms, everyone forgot about the smell of moonshine. The child's smile faded suddenly, and he looked at the room's occupants with solemn interest and curiosity, showing neither happiness nor fear. Mary walked over to him and held out her arms. He smiled and went to her straight away. She hugged him close and felt the familiar stinging in the back of her throat, as he wrapped his little arms around her neck and hugged her back. She buried her face in the front of his clean-smelling little shirt until the hot tears had subsided. Then she handed her son to her husband's waiting arms.

Sister beamed. "He's so right for you people! I knew he would be. Look, Anne, dear." She picked up the little girl. "That's your little brother. Would you like to talk to him? Wouldn't you like to say hello?"

Sonny grinned, put out his hand, and laughed out loud.

Anne smiled.

"What kind of soap do you use on the babies, Sister?" Mary asked, as they walked to the door. "Sonny smells so sweet and clean. I'd like to get some while we're in Sydney."

"I don't really know," Sister Frances smiled at everyone smiling around her. "We get it wholesale, and as far as I know, it's just called Baby Soap. You know," she smiled again, merrily this time, "I'd forgotten it had such a nice scent. I have these growths in my nose—polyps—or whatever they call them. I guess it's time I had them removed. I'm missing so many wonderful smells."

SISTER FRANCES THERESA WATCHED as the truck pulled away from the Home. Then she closed the door and leaned against it, laughing softly to herself. "So Joe Douglas is still drinking the moonshine!" She laughed again, remembering her father's comment on the old man. "He's jist doin' what the fancy folks do, but he ain't givin' the government a cut. And who can blame him? He's got little enough for himself." Her father had worked with Joe Douglas years and years before, when they were both young men working on the buildings at the Sydney steel plant. She wondered if she'd done right in not telling the old man who she was. She'd been only eleven when she'd last seen him.

Sister Frances shrugged and sniffed. Her nose did feel stuffed, but she could still detect the sweet smell of moonshine clinging in the room. She opened the window to let in the sharp December air, adjusted her veil that had been loosened in the wind, and went into the chapel for a quick prayer.

Our First Christmas

I WOKE WITH A START. The bedroom was full of shadows. A few hours ago, when I blew out the lamp, it had been pitch dark. Now I could make out the shapes of drawers and even the clothes rack across the room. Heavy clouds had hung low over the Glen all week, dumping their cargo of white snow. But the clouds had gone away while we slept, and now the moon hung high in the sky and the countryside was bathed in light. It seemed like a miracle. I heard footsteps on the landing.

"Jim," I whispered. "Wake up! The kids are up. I'm afraid Sonny might fall on the stairs. Those stairs are dangerous." I found myself shaking my head and mumbling. "We'll have to find the money somewhere for a banister." Every day since the children had come I'd worried about the stairs, and I used to like how narrow and steep they were.

"What time is it?" said Jim, shaking off my arm. "What's the matter with them?"

"It's Christmas, remember? They are looking for the presents Santa brought. It's four o'clock. You'd better hurry if you want to see their faces."

The floor was ice cold. I'd have to get the fire going right away.

"Be right there," said Jim, as he jumped out of bed and pulled on his trousers.

Together we tiptoed down the stairs, through the kitchen and into the front room. Two small figures in long flannelette nightgowns stood silent and still before the Christmas tree. The moonlight reflected from the ornaments and the tinsel on the tree created an aura about them.

"Angels!" Jim whispered.

I lit the lamp with shaking hands. The tree Jim had chosen was much larger than the ones we used to have in our little apartment in New York, and the decorations we'd bought with us were too few for such a large tree. The stores in Port Hood didn't carry anything so frivolous, and it was too late for a mail order when we came to decorate the tree. But Anne and Sonny couldn't see anything wrong.

"Look, Daddy!" I still pretended to be surprised. "Doesn't this big doll look like Anne? Do you suppose Santa meant it for her?" Anne's eyes were like blue whirlpools.

"I don't suppose Santa would leave a doll for a boy, now, do you princess?" said Jim lowering himself on his hunkers and putting his arm around her.

I took the doll from beside the tree and held it up. Anne chuckled with laughter, held out her arms, clutched the doll and held it close. It was nearly as tall as she was. I looked at Sonny.

"What did Santa bring for my big boy, I wonder?"

Sonny wasn't listening. He was looking at the tree.

"Look, Sonny, look! A fire engine! All for you. A big red fire engine!" Still Sonny paid no attention. Then suddenly he put out his hand and touched a golden ball hanging from the nearest branch. The ball quivered for a moment, then crashed to the floor, and shattered into tiny pieces. The corners of his mouth began to droop. But before Jim or I had time to speak Anne threw down her doll, grasped a blue and silver bell, threw it down on the floor, and danced up and down with glee.

"Anne! You musn't touch," I gasped, drawing her away. "They're not toys to play with. You musn't touch the tree. Just look at the pretty things."

With two of the biggest ornaments broken, our poor tree looked bare and forlorn. Jim took Anne by the hand and led her over to the armchair. He pointed to the bulging stockings hanging from either arm. I grabbed a small bear that stood guard over Sonny's stocking and held it close to his face trying to block his view of the tree. Slowly his eyes began to sparkle through the tears. Then holding out his little hands he took the bear and held it close to his chest. He laughed. This was the first time I had ever heard him laugh. The fire engine lay unnoticed under the tree. I got up from my knees and touched my man-child on the head. Then I made my way out into the kitchen.

DURING THE WEEK BETWEEN Christmas and the New Year every family in the Glen went visiting. Every man had to treat his neighbours to a drink. We would have to make at least two excursions—one up the road to the Beatons' and the MacTavishes' and the other down the road to Jim's father's place, Dougall's, J.J.'s, then up to Lawlors', and Ronnie's place over the hill. Jim thought we should start our visiting down the Glen. He harnessed Silver to the wood sleigh while I collected the old coats and comforters we had and piled them on behind. While I put on Sonny's coat Anne had taken one of the last ornaments left on the tree and insisted on hanging it on Silver's bridle. Jim waved away my protests and we took off in a whirl of snow. The mare was well fed and eager to run. As we turned off the Settlement Road we could see that there was no smoke coming from the chimney of Jim's father's house. They too must be visiting. We continued on our way down the river until Dougall's house came into view. No smoke came from his chimney either and there were no children playing in the yard.

"We'd best turn around and go back up to Lawlors'," said Jim, "they're all over at J.J.'s and drunk by now." He turned Silver around in the next gateway and we retraced our way up the hill and on towards Lawlors'. Our call at Lawlors' was a duty call, for Charles Lawlor was the big man up our end of the Glen. His house stood well back from the road and guarded by a carefully clipped spruce hedge. It was painted white; the only painted house for miles around. We swung in past the painted high-barred gate into the driveway. Silver took the turn with a burst of speed then slowed down to a walk up the steep slope to the house. Soon we heard singing. A Gaelic song—I knew the tune..."They had neither pole nor paddle So they could not cross the stream." Then a man's voice rang out, more heartily than melodious, describing the hero's frantic efforts to cross the water to the accompaniment of clapping hands beating out the rhythm. Then once again many voices joined in the chorus.

Margaret Lawlor met us at the door. She clasped the children in her arms and swept us into the parlour. She was a gentle soft-spoken little woman with twelve children of her own. We had barely time to take off our coats and rubbers before glasses were pressed into our hands. At Lawlors' each guest was given an individual glass. In the kitchen a gleaming stove hot from anthracite coal, and the air was filled with the aroma of spices from trays of cookies and cakes cooling in the pantry. Plates of turkey and pork sandwiches were laid out on long tables under the window. I was overwhelmed by the joy and hospitality around us. It was as if the framed blessing and prayers on the walls had all been brought to life. It was hard to believe, looking at Charles Lawlor now, that he could silence any one of his children, grown man or child, with a look.

The front room had been cleared for dancing. There was no musical instrument, but that didn't deter the dancers. As soon as a set finished, a voice started a faster tune, and before eight bars were sung the rest of the group joined in. A big strapping youth was pushed into the centre of the floor. He started a series of intricate steps. His feet moved like quicksilver, but his body remained rigid and his arms stiff. Soon our little Anne was jumping up and down trying to dance, and young Charlie Lawlor, a hefty lad in his early twenties led her on to the floor. She didn't know any of the tunes, but she had a good sense of rhythm. I was so proud of her. She looked so pretty, and her red-gold hair gleamed as her partner held her up and spun her round and round. I was so glad that I had been extravagant and made her a party dress especially for Christmas. It was blue velvet with lace collar and cuffs.

No one seemed to get tired, and no one got drunk. Three times we tried to leave but Margaret Lawlor wouldn't hear of it. At last I managed to convince her that we would have to be on our way. The whole family came to the door to see us off. They jammed the porch, waving their arms and calling out..."Merry Christmas! A Happy New Year!"

"Wasn't that something?" I said, as Silver took off at a sharp trot.

"Aye!" said Jim. "Stayed long'n we should have."

"What a fuss Margaret made when I wanted to leave."

"Awful nice people," Jim replied.

We had one more call to make.

"It'll have to be hello and good-bye at Ronnie's," said Jim. "Sun's losing her heat and it'll soon be dark. Don't want to be stumbling round in the dark feeding cows."

Jim pulled Silver's rein sharply to the left of the road. The mare knew her way home and wanted to turn the other way. Reluctantly she climbed up to the brow of the hill. At the crest we could see Ronnie's house.

"Look!" I cried. "They're all out in the snow."

"Fightin'," said Jim. "Must be the Roosters. Christina's people."

"The Roosters?"

"Aye! The Roosters!" said Jim with contempt. "When they're around, there's feathers flying. There's a whole settlement of them down the road from the church. With no one around to fight, they fight theyselves...and with anything that comes handy...fists, chairs, clubs, hair-pulling, anything at all."

"Let's not go in, Jim. We can wave from the road and turn around at the church. They'll never remember."

"No!" said Jim. "Can't do that. And I don't want to make another trip over—special. Get it over now."

Inside the house, everyone was drunk, even

the women. There was no sign of tea or any food. The men stopped fighting long enough to take the drink Jim offered them. One was passed out on the floor. We hadn't bothered to blanket Silver, and we left as quickly as we could.

"None of them will remember we were there," I said petulantly. "We should have gone past."

"WE know," said Jim, firmly.

"Do we have time to run in and give old William Barnes a drink?" I said, looking at the tall gaunt house that hadn't a single light shining through the windows. "It's Christmas, and that poor old man probably won't have any callers at all."

"We'll do that," said Jim. "We'll stay long enough to give him a drink, and that's all."

The children were fast asleep and warm. I went into the house while Jim tied up the mare. The old man didn't hear me enter the kitchen. He sat huddled over the stove, wrapped in an old ragged coat, a cap pulled down over his ears, and his booted feet in the oven. The whole room was hazy with smoke that poured from a crack on the stove top and a loose connection in the chimney pipe. The window was shrouded with limp shreds of curtaining that showed traces of having once been crisp and gay. An unlit lamp, the bowl empty and the funnel caked in soot, a grimy glass of water, and a flickering lantern stood on the table. The old man neither heard me, nor seemed to see me as I moved around.

"Don't shut the door," I called out to Jim when I heard his steps in the porch.

"Why the hell not?" Jim called back. "Want to freeze everyone out?"

"Leave it open. Just for a minute to let the smoke out."

As the air cleared, Jim looked around. I saw him looking at the place beside the stove where marks on the wall showed that wood had been stacked there in days gone by. On the floor lay a single piece of wood, about two feet in length and an inch in diameter. I raised the lid of the stove and motioned Jim to look. Inside, a half-burned chunk of wood encrusted with mud lay smouldering. Jim bent down and shook the old man gently, then took the bottle out of his pocket and held it up for him to see. The old eyes grew wide with excitement. He drank thirstily, but when we shouted "Merry Christmas," he only laughed foolishly, his eyes blank and without expression.

"He doesn't know he's alive," I whispered.

"He don't have any wood," Jim whispered. "Must be some, some place."

"Doesn't he have any relatives?"

"There a nephew or cousin or something in the village, but they don't pay him no mind. Never come out to see how he's doing. I'll take a look around and see if I can find wood for tonight."

Jim stopped at the door.

"Now we can't take him home, so don't try and be a Florence Nightingale, or something. Tomorrow, maybe, we can do something else...even if he is so mean that he wouldn't give his mother a nickel, and her starving to death."

"But we can't leave him to die alone at Christmas!" I protested.

"Now you stay here. I won't be a minute," said Jim, as he went out.

I picked up the lantern and found the pantry. The shelves were bare. There was no bread, nothing in the house. Jim sooned returned with an armful of odds and ends of wood.

"Make him a cup of tea," said Jim, throwing the wood into the stove.

"I can't, Jim. I've looked everywhere and there isn't any food in the house. Not even a pinch of tea. It's too late to go home and get some, but we can leave the fruitcake and apples that are in the shoe box on the sleigh."

We left the cake and the apples with old William. Silver needed no urging, she was anxious as we were to get home. The sun had just disappeared over the far hills, and the light was fading fast. Jim would have to feed the animals by lantern light.

We heard the sleigh bells ahead before we saw Charlie Lawlor, standing spraddle-legged on his sleigh, towering over his mare. Jim hailed him, and reined Silver to a halt. We told Charlie what we had seen.

"Hmmm!" said Charlie. "D'ye think if I took him some potatoes and turnips, he'd have the sense to cook 'em? I'd best take a run up anyways."

"Well, that's our good deed for today," I said, as the sleigh moved off.

"If the neighbours are true to form, by the time Charlie makes his rounds tonight the old man'll have everyone in the Glen calling with their hands full before the week's out," said Jim, giving Silver a flick with the reins.

"What makes you think that?" I asked.

"Oh! Guessin'!" said Jim with a broad smile. "Margaret Lawlor'll make it her business to see that the relatives find out that the neighbours are feeding poor William, and they'll find a way of getting him away—him having all that money. I didn't see hide nor hair of his old dog. He must've breathed his last."

IT WAS GOOD TO GET HOME. I was cold and tired. What a Christmas it had been! I put the children to bed while Jim unloaded the sleigh and fed the animals. I soon had the fire going and the kettle singing on the stove. I looked out of the kitchen window. There was a full moon, and the snow was bathed in golden light. I could see Jim's lantern moving inside the barn.

"Mary! Come here!" It was Jim calling. "I got something to show ye!"

I pulled on my coat and boots, and ran out into the barn.

"Look!" said Jim, pointing to a heap of straw.

There stood a newborn calf, as frisky as a speckled trout. As soon as he saw me he darted over to his mother, old Star, who stood there, placid and content, chewing her cud.

"No need to ask is she all right," said Jim, throwing her an extra ration of hay. "Been a while since that feller came. Must've happened an hour or so after we left."

"Oh Jim! Isn't he a beauty! He's the best Christmas present I ever had. But I have something better than any gift this Christmas, Jim."

"An' what's that?"

"It just came to me now. Here we are, with our own home, our own land, two lovely children, good health, good food and good neighbours. This is the best Christmas I ever had. Ever, ever, ever!"

Gothic Neighbours

WHEN I FIRST CAME TO THE GLEN there had been seven members of the MacTavish family living up the Settlement Road. Lauchie, the eldest, Joe, Andy, John, deaf and dumb Dave, their only sister, Rose, and her twenty-year-old son, Dan.

Joe and Andy were the first to leave. One day they came home sick, hungry and dirty after four days drinking, and Lauchie told them to go and earn their own keep.

Then there was Francis; who his parents were no one knew, but curious neighbours made it their business to search him out. They never got close enough to see more than a face at the loft window, a fleeting shadow with snowy beard and a mane of hoary silk disappearing into the woods. Sure of their ground now, they went to the priest and pounded out the carpet in the vestry behind the altar. The next day the good Father drove out to the MacTavishes. It took a big man to hold Francis, the wild one, now forty years of age or more, while the priest gave him his blessing and cleansed him of original sin.

There had been many stories after that. One dark and stormy night (so it was said), poor Francis took a pain and expired and so his mortality had finally to be recognized. Reluctant to share his knowledge with his neighbours, Lauchie approached a man he felt committed to keep his secret—a cousin, Matt MacInnes; besides, Matt had a truck! Late that night, wringing wet and trembling, Lauchie arrived at Matt's house, across the river.

"I thought he must be drunk or something, him walking and it storming like it was." No one could stop Matt telling the story after a couple of drinks. "But he said Francis had died, ye know, and he had to get a box to bury him in. He wanted to know would I take him to Sandy's the coffin maker over in Glen Murray. I wasn't even dressed, but I put me clothes on and went with him. He didn't say no word till we got to the top of the hill, then he said, 'For God's sake, Matt, don't let on who it is we're gitting the box for.'"

When Rose gave birth to her first illegitimate son—she had three—her father accused old Henry MacLeod. Old Henry "the Dirty" as he was called, acknowledged his guilt, raised the boy, and when he died willed his farm to him, now only an overgrown clearing in the woods. Rose gave her second son, whose sire no one had a mind to guess at, away to foster parents; last of all came Dan, whom she kept and named Dan Beaton, letting it be known that Harold Beaton was the father. Harold denied having any part of it, but Dan remained a Beaton until he was old enough to know better, at which time he renamed himself Dan MacTavish.

It happened this way. Rose had hidden Dan's bottle of bush whiskey while he sat in a drunken stupor. His long hair fell down across his forehead almost into a string of mucous that hung from his nose, left there unattached after a sneeze.

Dan always sneezed in his stupors and wet himself until pools formed underneath his chair that filled one mop at least, and sometimes two or more. Dan had never been known to shout, argue or use his towering strength against man or beast in the whole of his twenty years, but when Rose lost her temper and told him what she thought of him, and who his father was, he grabbed her throat and tried to bash her brains out against the steel bowl of the cream separator. Rose was not small and she struggled with all her strength.

Out in the barn Dave finished his chores and sauntered back to the house and the warmth of the fire. Pushing open the door of the back porch he saw Dan, gripping Rose's throat with a ferocity that whitened his fingers. Then with the fury of a plucked peacock Dave, slim and feather-light, threw himself at Dan in such a frenzy that Dan's grip relaxed. Rose took to her heels. Her time was seven minutes to the half-mile end. There at Beatons' she told her tale, and with the help of Harold, Joe, and the buggy she made her exit from the farm and from the Glen.

Dave

MARY COULDN'T BELIEVE how anybody could think that Dave wasn't an intelligent human being. His own brother, Lauchie, always spoke of him as being stupid and senseless but Mary had noticed, on many occasions when there was a problem to be solved on the farm and neighbours came to offer their experience, that it would be Dave's ingenuity and energy that found a solution. To put a man such as Dave "a-hide" as if he were some penance cast upon his parents and family seemed inhuman to Mary. She knew that there was nothing wrong with Dave's hearing. She had heard him tap his toes rhythmically to the radio or scamper to a window minutes before anyone else heard a sound, sometimes to identify a rig going along the road and find out whether it was going on up to his place or turning into the yard. He would utter ugly little sounds but Mary reasoned that since he could hear so well he could also be taught to speak.

One day, Lauchie decided to take a trip into town and he left Dave at home alone. Mary had just seen Lauchie and his rig go down the road when another figure, coming from the same direction, walked up into the yard. It was Dave. He knocked at the door and made signs that he wanted an egg. Mary called him in and cooked him eggs and gave him tea; but when he had finished he made no sign of wanting to leave and since he looked so lonesome, Mary left her washing and sat down at the table beside him. She soon exhausted the small number of signs that she knew and in a very short time she and Dave found themselves staring out the window. Then Dave idly fingered a pencil Mary had left on the table when she had finished writing the laying records of her hens. Suddenly aware of what his hands were doing, he took an empty envelope torn open from yesterday's mail and, bending down until his face almost touched the pencil, he began to move his fingers laboriously.

After several minutes and beaming with pride, he passed the envelope across to Mary. On the envelope Dave had written...DAVE MACTAVISH—the outline of each letter clear and strong. Mary had no difficulty in showing her surprise or in giving her praise. Once more Dave grasped the envelope and with more relaxed and sure movements he began to write numbers—all of them from one to a hundred. After writing each he raised a corresponding number of fingers on his left hand. A closed fist stood for ten, so three jerks of a closed fist followed by three pointed fingers meant thirty-three...and so he counted until he reached one hundred and then he began to really show off!

Without ever standing upright, his shoulders still bent as they had been over the table, he crossed the floor to the clock. He showed the time Lauchie had left home and when he was expected back; the time he himself had left—which was ten minutes later; and the time he had spent on the road. Having elicited astonishment and admiration from Mary, he again crossed the floor, his back still bent, to a calendar hanging on the wall. He pointed out all the Holy Days of Obligation for the entire year and the compulsory confession and Communion that preceded each day, which he explained by drawing his hand across his throat to indicate a clerical collar then moving his jaw to mime the movements of eating. He went still further, he turned the leaves of the calendar, and pointed out the Fast Days. No one could doubt the meaning of his fingers to the lips, the negative shake of the head, and no one could doubt Dave's knowledge of his subject.

Mary knew that Dave always carried a rosary in his pocket for she had watched him strike off bead by bead as though he knew the prayers for every one. But Dave had not finished his demonstration. He showed Mary that he must receive Communion twice yearly, at Easter and Christmas, or he would die. Whether it had been Rose, his mother, before she left for Boston, or his grandmother who had taught him, Mary didn't know; but it was not for her to correct their teaching.

Dave's absolution and blessing were obtained in a very simple way. Lauchie (now that Rose was gone) would go first into the confession, explain

Dave's affliction to the priest, then send in Dave directly. After receiving absolution, Dave would kneel at the altar and receive his Host, his mind at peace until the next Day of Obligation.

IT WAS PAST NOON on Easter Saturday. Lent was over and Mary was preparing for Easter. The smell of baking pies filled the house. Cookies, cakes and spicy pies were cooling in the pantry and four golden loaves from white flour stood on the rack; now, all she had to do was bake a raisin bread, left to the last until the pans had cooled. She stood before the kitchen window patting the raised dough into rounded loaves...outside the sky was dark, and for an hour or more there had been sheets of drenching rain falling...it wasn't fit for a man or beast to be out and yet advancing with great strides towards the house was a hatless figure and between the long strings of drenched hair she recognized Dave's tragic face. He bounded through the door without a knock or any sign of apology. He stood before Mary, his eyes deploring his affliction—he darted to the calendar and back again, his hands and fingers moving in grotesque gyrations, sounds sludged through his trembling lips.

When her first terror had passed, Mary stood waiting for her pounding heart to subside. Then she gently grasped Dave's arm and smiling, made him understand that he must calm himself if she were to understand what he was trying to tell her. Gradually the frenzy, the fire left his eyes and in place of fire were ashes, that spoke more eloquently than words for this soul's tribulation. By nudging Dave on slowly from one gesture to another Mary made out his story.

Lauchie had been celebrating the coming of Easter for a week, and he showed no signs of being sober for the solemnity of Easter—he was, at this very moment, fast asleep in the kitchen. Dave made frantic signs of blessing, and then pantomimed a priest standing over an open grave.... Dave believed that he would die physically as well as spiritually if he did not receive Communion on Easter Sunday!

Anger came over Mary like a torrent; she threw on her coat and ran to the barn to find Joe, but he had no comfort to give her.

"You'd better keep your nose out of it," he said. "Lauchie will think you have a hell of a nerve buttin' into his business. Can't you tell Dave something different?"

"I'm going back with Dave whether you come or not, come and see for yourself the state he's in."

"No, I'm not going," said Joe, without moving a step, "and I don't think you should either."

Joe understood the minds and the ways of his people better than Mary.

Next morning the worshippers had filled the altar rails again and again but among the last to come forwards was a swollen-faced and watery-eyed Lauchie and a smiling Dave.

The Raid on the Promised Land

It WAS AN APRIL SUNDAY—a bright day with just enough crust on the snow to make good sledding—a perfect day, said Jim Douglas, to visit Lauchie MacTavish up the Settlement Road. The old folks had died a few years before, and the boys, all of them bachelors, had sent for Lauchie to come home. They wrote that there was nobody to look after "The Dummy," unless he'd come home and do it. Of course, it was only an excuse to get him home to look out for them all. But he did come, for the sake of his brother Dave, born deaf and condemned to a world of gestures and his own brand of sign language, though Dave was wiser and cannier than most of his brothers. And now Lauchie was getting just like the rest of them, and just as likely not to get married. They were none of them much to look at.

Jim liked his Sundays with Mary and the kids. They gave him a break from the barn and a chance to tell her old stories about the Glen and its people. He knew she felt strange among them, an outsider among the women—and that she often found it easier to get along with the men. They all called her "the woman from away," until they got to know her. Then she was just Mary.

On their way to Lauchie's, they passed a splendid stand of pine and maple, the trees so huge and towering that Mary wondered aloud why they had never been cut.

"That's The Promised Land!" Jim chuckled.

"The Promised Land! What does that mean?" asked Mary, pleased at the prospect of another story, another piece in the history of her adopted community.

"Well," began Jim, equally pleased to tell the story. "For years there's been a running feud between the Beatons and the MacTavishes over that strip of land. It's maybe three generations ago that old man MacTavish was sent foolish by a fit of good humour—likely brought on by his latest brew. Anyhow, he announced that he was giving that strip as a bridal gift to his daughter Sarah, who was going to marry one of the Beaton boys. The wedding took place all right, but the girl died with her first baby. Old MacTavish then claimed that her death invalidated the transfer of the land. But Old Beaton claimed just as stubbornly that a gift was a gift.

"To add insult to injury, young Beaton took himself a new wife, Millie Doyle, an outsider from three glens away. Well, the Doyle girl was a little luckier. She had three boys, one right after the other, before she followed Sarah MacTavish to the grave. Poor Beaton was in rough straits. It was hard enough to find a wife, but three kids and his record—nobody at all would bite.

"The last straw was the sewing machine. The MacTavish girl took her sewing machine with her over the brush fence, but when she died, the sewing machine stayed over. Time after time, Old Man MacTavish claimed that since there was no woman in the Beaton house any more, they had no use for the sewing machine. But the machine stayed. With his dying breath, Old Man Beaton told his sons to keep it and lock it.

"Now, it's still in the place where she put it, locked up tight. But the key to it's lost. And there's The Promised Land. You see it yourself—virgin forest, wonderful trees that nobody'll cut because nobody'll agree on who owns them. It's kind of a legend here. But they share it—now nobody cares so much who owns it. They run moonshine in it—often together."

Jim looked at his wife with a wry smile.

Mary laughed at the story. She liked her husband's tales about the old days. Usually he was too busy or too tired to talk at all. Sunday was her favourite day of the week.

WHEN JIM AND MARY ENTERED the MacTavish house, they nearly tumbled into a gaping hole in the kitchen floor. Lauchie's black head popped cheerfully out of it to greet them. "Take a chair," he said. "I'll be through an' up with ye in a minute. Jist after gittin' some potatoes fer beer."

His eyes were gleaming in a way that told its own story. In the Glen, there were three stages in drinking—"wasn't sufferin' any," "feelin' good," and "full." Lauchie wasn't sufferin' any.

Mary looked around. A queer thing on the table caught her eye. She picked it up. It looked like a home-made curry comb for an over-sized grizzly. Rows of nails had been driven through a piece of wood about a foot long, and bristled savagely on the other side. She held it up to Jim in bewilderment.

"It's a scraper for potatoes," he whispered.

She looked more puzzled.

"Fer moonshine." Only his lips moved on his indrawn breath.

Lauchie's shoulders and torso followed his head up from the cellar. He heaved a bucket of potatoes onto the kitchen floor. Then he climbed up the ladder and covered the hole with a square of flooring. Satisfied that the hole was safe again, he picked up the bucket and sat down at the table.

"I got the 'credentials' at the Co-op yesterday," he said. "Dan and John drunk the last the day before, yeast and all, when I wass in town, and it still workin'. That near finished it." He waggled his head at Mary. "I wassn't gonna make any more, but then I like a little sip now and again, an' it costs too much to buy. Too bad ye didna git here a minute sooner." He slid his thumb up his finger, measuring the depth of a good drink, and grinned roguishly at them. "There wass that much left, but I jist finished it 'fore ye came in."

"When you make the run, could I watch?" Mary blurted, taking care not to look at Jim, who was confounded by her breach of good manners and rose red-faced and spluttering apologies for her. Women never went near a still, and men didn't ask to watch.

Lauchie seemed not to notice Jim's embarrassment. "Sure," he said. "Why not? Just hand me the scraper, would ye?"

He was about to drag a potato across the bristle of nails, when he stopped and grinned foolishly. "I s'pose I'd best rub some of the dirt off 'fore I do that," he said.

He went into the pantry and brought back a battered white enamel dishpan, half full of water. He threw in as many potatoes as the pan would hold, and washed them, without brush or cloth, sloshing the water like a miner panning for gold. When he finished them all, he picked up the scraper and this time scraped potato after potato until he had a bucket full of blackened pulp.

"Might as well git goin'," said Lauchie, picking up the bucket. "You bring the molasses, will ye, Jim?"

They followed him down behind the barn to a tiny clearing in the woods which was cut by a narrow, fast-moving brook. On its near bank stood a squat, thick barrel—empty. To the right of the barrel, a ring of dead ashes blackened the snow.

Lauchie started to gather kindling and wood for the fire.

"The dry stuff iss best," he said, dropping a heavy chunk that was too green. "Wet stuff makes a hell of a smoke. Hangs low over the trees. Like a black flag. Sign fer the Mounties to come checkin'."

Once the fire was blazing, Lauchie filled a big blackened pot with brook water and set it on a steel contraption that stretched across the fire between two rocks. The water was boiling in no time. Lauchie tipped the pot into the barrel, added the potato pulp, and tested the temperature of the mash on his wrist. It was right. He took five cakes of yeast from his pants pocket, crumbled them between his fingers, and dropped them into the mash. Then he crossed the clearing and brought back a sturdy maple branch, smooth and stained from frequent use. This he plunged into the barrel and stirred until the ingredients were well mixed. He poured in the black molasses and stirred again. Satisfied, he draped an old feed bag over the barrel and shovelled wet sand on the fire, stirring it well into the ashes. Then he arranged twigs and leaves over the barrel until it looked like a tree stump.

"There! Beer's set," he said proudly. "We'll move 'er into the stable tonight after dark. Keep 'er warm till she's done."

Lauchie ran a hand over his head. "Well," he said, "that's all we can do now for a week or ten days, till she quits workin'."

Mary and Jim left for home.

THE FOLLOWING SUNDAY, they were on the

road before dawn. Lauchie had stopped by Saturday to say the beer was ready and he'd be doing the run about daybreak. The crust on the snow was still hard and the coral sunset of the evening before had promised a warm day. As they pulled the mare up at the MacTavish house, Dave darted from the door and jumped on the sleigh, grinning just like Lauchie. He gave the rein a sharp tug. The mare about-faced and retraced her steps to The Promised Land. Dave signalled to stop. Then he leaped from the sleigh to the edge of the road and poked around the sodden undergrowth.

Jim jumped out after Dave and searched the snow for tracks. He found none. Dave nervously checked up and down the road again and fished a long plank from the undergrowth. Then he grabbed Jim by the shoulder, pointed up and down the road, put his hand to his eyes, slapped Jim on the shoulder where an RCMP badge would be and marked out the position of the Mountie's strap. Jim understood his assignment exactly.

With another cautionary glance up and down the road, Dave picked up the plank. He laid the near end of it on top of a flat boulder, well above the snow at the edge of the road, then aimed the other end at a huge tree stump. Gently, his face full of sober concern, he let it down. Again he made worried signals. They understood. They had to walk along the plank—and very carefully.

"Taking no chances, are they?" said Mary.

"Gonna make damn sure no Mountie'll catch

'em," Jim answered. "Not by followin' their tracks into the woods, anyways."

Dave was as solemn in his care as a penitent receiving the last rites. They filed in behind him, obeying his urgent signals. As soon as they were across the plank, he positioned it again, while they stood waiting on another stump. Once more they stepped to the end of the plank, and once more Dave positioned it. And so they proceeded, again and again, until they were deep into the woods and completely screened from the road.

Dave grinned and pointed to a well-travelled path. Jim turned to follow it, but once more Dave seized his arm. Using both hands, he mimed the driving of a horse until Jim nodded his understanding. Then he swung his arm in the direction of the MacTavish house and pointed at the sun just rising over the dark trees. Jim nodded again as Dave turned in a circle until his arm pointed straight up, indicating that he would be back at noon. He grinned and pointed at the path into the woods. Then he picked up the plank, and left.

Jim and Mary hadn't far to go. Soon they smelled smoke, and shortly afterwards they saw the fire. It was in a clearing, quite a sizable clearing, but the thick woods and giant trees made it seem small. They saw Lauchie approaching the crackling fire with a bucket of water in either hand. He nodded, emptied the water into the barrel next to the fire, and turned to them.

"Ye didna have trouble understandin' Dave,

did ye? Shoulda told ye the lay-out yesterday. I fergot."

He was making polite chat, and both Mary and Jim knew it. The location of any still was kept as secret as the sins of the confessional.

Harold Beaton came up behind Lauchie with two more buckets of water. He was unshaven and a little shaky. His Saturday night had not been dry, and his rumpled trousers looked slept in. But he nodded affably to Jim and Mary before he sloshed the water into the barrel. An unwritten law dictated that any man near a still had to take a hand in running it. Harold was familiar with his job and needed no instructions.

"John and Jim Beaton iss off gittin' dry wood," Lauchie grinned. "Wanna give a hand makin' some dough to plug them holes. More iss goin' up in steam than iss goin' down through the worm."

Both men set off towards the woods, leaving Mary to stare at the contraption over the fire. She had never seen its like. An old copper washboiler had been positioned on heavy steel bars. A round hole roughly six inches across had been cut in the center of the lid. Soldered to this was what Jim had described as the collar, into which tapered a copper elbow. The fogs of steam escaping from the soot-blackened boiler made the contrivance look like a devil's cauldron.

Lauchie and Jim came back with fistfuls of flour and water dough. Steam was still rising from every joint. If Lauchie was going to save his moonshine, those leaks would have to be doughed up fast. Lauchie started patching the joints where the steam was escaping, and Jim kept handing him gobs of sticky dough, all the while joking over the number of cracks and holes that had to be patched.

"Ach! Well!" said Lauchie. "It iss good enough. There's so many cracks in it the Mounties'd be thinkin' it's only fit fer boilin' water in fer scaldin' hogs when yer butcherin'. Truth iss, it's hardly tight enough even fer that." His little eyes crinkled with laughter.

Mary stepped closer and peered into the water barrel. There the straight tubing narrowed to a one inch copper pipe that spiralled all the way down through the water. This was the coil or "worm" she'd been told about. The steam in the coil condensed as it wound through the cold water. Then it dripped from the bottom, where a hole had been bored in the barrel to allow the end of the coil to come out. A feed bag wrapped around the copper spout kept the barrel leak to a slow drip. Beneath the spout itself, a clear pungent liquid trickled steadily into a dipper that was filled to the brim and beginning to overflow.

"Lauchie, you'll lose some if you don't come quick," said Mary. "Should I empty it?" She was eager for a job.

Lauchie dropped the urgent task of doughing to pick up the full dipper. He replaced it with a handleless china cup, so that not a drop should be lost while he emptied the dipper into a gallon jug. Then, realizing that Mary had wanted to do it, he tried to make amends.

"Would ye be after tryin' it?" His eyes blinked merrily. "Ye first, Jim. And ye too, Mary. We've been havin' a little taste each time we changed the cup. T'iss not bad! Me grandfather got the recipe out of an old Temperance book, y'know."

"A book!" said Mary. "Imagine that! Would you bring it down to me sometime. I'd like to see it. This stuff's good!"

"Mary!" Jim shook his head. "Fer Pete's sake!"

"She iss jist kiddin'," chuckled Lauchie. "I'll bring it. I know jist where it iss. That's all right, Jim."

When the whole job was done, Lauchie held up a quart bottle half full of the last drops.

"Don't know what I'm botherin' to save this fer," he said. "It's a cinch I won't be usin' it."

"Why not, Lauchie?" Mary laughed, feeling warm from the moonshine.

"They're tailin's to start the next run with. But I won't be makin' it though. This batch'll do me." His speech was getting blurred, and he carefully placed the bottle beside the jug under a silver birch and eased himself down for another little sip.

Lauchie saw Dave coming into a clearing and shied like a skittish horse. He fumbled for the gallon jug, hastily stumbled to his feet, and stood in front of his brother grinning. Dave's eyes moved from one man to another with a grin of his own, then stopped on Mary. He clucked his tongue and drew circles at his temple with a forefinger. Everyone laughed heartily at the silent comment. Mary joined them.

Lauchie knocked the fixtures loose from the coil. Dave emptied the blackpot and took off with it in another direction. The fire was doused. Barrel, metal grill and buckets were whisked out of sight. When they started back to the sleigh, Lauchie had trouble walking straight; and he twice staggered off the path into the snow. Dave was frowning deeply by the time they reached the plank.

There, quick as a cat, Dave pounced on Lauchie and carried him, jug and all, across the first plank—and across every succeeding one. Lauchie's arms stopped flailing after the first. At last they were all in the sleigh. The snow between the road and the blackpot was still not cut.

A very dry and sober Lauchie kept his promise and brought Mary the Temperance book later that week. It was very old, its faded green cover marked and ringed. But there, on page twelve, right after a sermon on the perils of tobacco, wine and ribaldry, was a complete guide to the distillation of hard liquor from molasses and potatoes. Mary had been the first woman in The Promised Land, indeed the only one to see a "run." And then Lauchie said he was "going on the wagon."

THE STILL WAS PASSED OVER to Lauchie's brother John, who looked enough like "The Dummy" to be a twin, but lacked his sense. John calculated that the washboiler wasn't big enough for what he had in mind, so he went to Mac, the blacksmith in the next village, and got him to rig up a forty-five-gallon steel drum. Together they cut a round hole in the top and soldered the connecting parts steam tight. Both were "full" when the job was done, and Mac lurched home to his wife. The "pay" he'd accepted was sweeter going down than coming up; and for two days he cradled his head, while his wife scrubbed up the messes and railed at his stupidity and the evils of moonshine.

Lauchie was giving Jim Douglas a day at the threshing when John borrowed his horse and wagon to cart the drum the twelve miles to The Promised Land. On the way home, he picked up enough yeast cake and molasses to start his business. John was figuring his profit and counting the friends he could expect as customers as he let the horse carry him home. His figuring ignored the blacksmith's wife, who had watched his retreating shape with taut lips.

Lauchie grinned when Jim said cautiously, "He's into a hornet's nest there. She's death on liquor. She'd squeal in a minute."

"He took my rig t'git that damn drum. They'll all be thinkin' now it's me that owns it." Lauchie stuck a straw between his teeth and chewed. "I s'pose we'd be obliged to warn him though."

"Too bad he won't ever give a fella a sip," said Jim.

"He iss meanin' t'sell it." Lauchie's voice was dry.

ONE SOGGY DAY that September, in spite of the clay that clogged the wheels of every moving vehicle to their hubs, a Mountie turned at the crossroads and slogged his way down the Settlement Road. Twice in a week, he braved the deepening ruts, and both times he stopped to talk to Jim Douglas.

"What did he want?" asked Mary.

"Nothing much," said Jim.

"Well, I hope he got it then."

"I don't know if he did or not," Jim chuckled.

The next day Jim took Mary and Lauchie to town for groceries and got the truck stuck to its axles in mud.

"Damn it all!" he growled. "The Mountie got through yesterday."

"Yiss?" Lauchie cocked a curious eyebrow. "And what time was that, Jim?"

"Two—maybe three o'clock."

"We thought he might be looking for John's blackpot," said Mary.

"The slink!" Lauchie grinned, then frowned.

The men were collecting stones to put under the truck's tires.

"When I can't get through with the truck," Jim fumed, "I don't see how he made it with that car of his, and it so low."

"They got good cars," said Lauchie. "The best they make."

"Ye'd best tell John, so he'll know."

"Y' can't talk t' John. Too pig-headed. Y'know how he iss. Jist rollin' his makin's and smokin', and doin' whatever suits him. Never givin' a thought to the Mounties bein' after 'im."

"Tell 'im anyways," said Jim.

"I had an idea something wass up," said Lauchie, collecting more rocks. "Dave wass gabblin' somethin'. Thought he seed tracks at the gate, but I figured he wass seein' things. Musta been that Mountie. Wass there just one in the car?"

"I couldn't see very good." Jim was cursing the road and the mud. "But I think there was only one."

"I wonder what took 'im up." Lauchie pondered, shoving another rock under the wheel. "Ye didna see 'im go back?"

"Damn well, he didn't come back over this road." Jim was furious and getting muddier by the minute. "We'll have to cut a pole to lever up that axle if we're gonna git out today."

By the time the truck was under way again, both men were mud-caked to the knees, and splattered all over. Only the back of Jim's shirt was the clean blue plaid he'd set out in that morning. Neither man had forgotten the Mountie.

WHEN THEY GOT BACK FROM TOWN, Lauchie went home on foot, and Jim went to the barn to check on a cow that was due to freshen. He heard the grumble of a motor and ran to the dung window to get a clearer view of the car and its driver. The Mountie, confident as a rooster, was managing the ruts, but with less ease than before. Jim could hear the tires growling. He snickered quietly to himself as he went back to shovelling the stable.

In the house, Mary was getting supper ready and feeding the children; but she too was watching the road and saw the Mountie's car come struggling through the mud.

When Jim came in to eat, he said, "That fella'll be stuck before long, and he'll be after help from the MacTavishes—or me. A little more mud on my clothes mightn't be a bad investment fer him to leave us be."

After supper, Jim waited expectantly for a knock. He read the paper while Mary darned mitts. Outside, the night was black as a hobo's pocket. No sound broke the rain's steady rumble.

"Let's go to bed, Mary," Jim said at nine o'clock.

Upstairs Mary lay half awake, listening to the rain and her husband's snoring. Suddenly she heard pounding on the door.

Startled, she looked at the time. Ten o'clock! Who would drag people from their beds at this hour?

She nudged Jim. He stopped snoring and rolled over. She got out of bed and ran down the stairs.

A harsh voice stabbed the night.

"Open up! I'm the RCMP. My car's stuck up the road and I want Mr. Douglas to pull me out."

Jim came running down the stairs in his sock feet, still buttoning his fly.

"Be with you soon's I get my coat," he called out. To Mary, he whispered, "I figured he'd get stuck, but at the last, I thought he must've made it or got the MacTavishes to give 'im a hand."

It was three hours before Jim came back.

"Where was he stuck?" asked Mary.

"In a bog up between here and Lauchie's. He said he'd been stuck there the whole time."

"Did he mention his business?"

"Somethin' about a report there'd been sheep stealin'. Balls! Nobody up there with sheep!"

"What a night to be stuck so long!"

"Must be hellish anxious to get that blackpot—if that's what he's after. Said the Department would pay me and asked me how much. Then 'fore I could git a word out, he said they only paid three dollars, and that I'd get a cheque." Jim was peeved. "I wouldn't turn out this time o' night for ten dollars, but what can ye do? Law says you have to help 'em."

"Did you get the money?"

"NO! I have to sign a paper."

"Where was the bog he was stuck in?"

"Up by The Promised Land."

"The Promised Land! The cheapskate! You were gone three hours in this downpour!"

"I know! I know! Let's go to bed."

TWO DAYS LATER, the Mountie was back, on foot, looking for Jim's signature. He stayed for an hour at the barn. Mary watched him from the window waving his hands. He looked to be talking about ruts and car wheels, and all the while Jim held the paper, ready to sign. Then she saw him take the pen and the paper from Jim and walk away. Later Jim told her that he never once mentioned the MacTavishes or the Beatons or the stolen sheep.

Jim Beaton and Lauchie drove up at sunset with the mare and wagon. They were on the way to pick up their mail, and offered to get Mary's and Jim's too.

"Mountie was here agin today." Jim told the whole story. "He's after John, sure'n hell. Ye better tell 'im."

"I told 'im already, and he won't do nothin' but smoke." Lauchie leaned back on the kitchen chair. "Too cocky, he iss. Says he'll not get caught in the rain, 'cause the roads iss too muddy fer the Mounties nor nobody else t'git through."

"Well, I'm tellin' ye," put in Jim Beaton, "there's somethin' in them woods. I could tell by the mare. When we come by, she jumped and shied t' the other side of the road. Jenny don't git scared like that fer nothing." His head snapped down, forcing his chin even further into the folds of loose skin above his collar. "That Mountie is up in them woods right now."

"John's makin' noises 'bout doin' a run in the morning." Lauchie looked worried. "I told him t' leave it alone. Jist not t' go near at all. Tellin's iss one thing. What he'll do iss another. He's got big ideas, and it's hard t' change his mind."

"Well," said Mary, "tell him about this. That Mountie's after John, and he won't stop till he gets him. You never got so much attention before, not from the Mounties."

"He's determined all right," Jim agreed, shaking his head. A grin was starting to twitch at the corners of his mouth. "Reminds me of Father Murphy. Remember him, Lauchie?"

"Remember him!" Lauchie laughed aloud. "It's me that does."

"He used to be at yer place a lot. Ever catch you?"

"Oh, yeh!" Lauchie was enjoying himself. "Came out once with—what's his name, now?" He snapped his fingers as if to pluck the name from the air. "You know his name, Jim. The Mountie—"

"Lynch?" offered Jim.

"That's him! Lynch! Drove up one Sunday, and the yard full of rigs. Yer old man was there, and mine too."

"And did he git anything?"

"Noooooo! Everything got cleaned up the minute we seed 'em turnin' in the gate. They couldna find even a smell. When they wass leavin' the Father told me—'Yer not foolin' me, Lauchie, I'll get ye yet!' But he never did."

The men laughed.

"Remember old Lexie MacQuarrie?" asked Jim.

Lauchie looked puzzled.

"Lived up on the ridge. Remember? Her husband was Angus, and they had a whole raft o' kids."

"Yiss, yiss," Lauchie grinned. "I remember them now."

"And did ye hear what she told Father Murphy about Angus's blackpot?"

"Must've heard. Yiss, I remember somethin'. But what was it?"

"Father Murphy went to the house and old Lexie came to the door. Him and the Mountie'd been searchin' the woods lookin' fer Angus's blackpot. Lexie knew about them bein' on the farm soon's they set foot on the place. When the Father asked where Angus was, she said she didn't know. Then the nosey old bugger up and asked her right out, 'Well, where's Angus's blackpot, then?' Old Lexie, she didn't care fer nothin' y'know. She jist said—'Ye wanna see Angus's blackpot, Father? Well, then! Whatta ya know!' An' she put on that awful grin, whirled around, bent down, her skirt clean over her head, and stuck her big fat arse right in his face. 'There's Angus's blackpot fer ye, Father!'"

The men laughed aloud, then fell silent.

"Ah, yiss," Jim Beaton chuckled. "Yiss, yiss, I remember now."

"Anyways, I told John," said Lauchie. "And if the stubborn mule won't be payin' no mind at all, I can't help it."

"But he will when you tell him about tonight," said Mary.

"Nothin' he can do," said Jim. "If the Mountie's there now."

"No—not much," Lauchie spoke up quickly. "But I'm gonna tell 'im strong to let that beer alone—stay away altogether. It iss all worked out, ye know, and ready to run. John iss after braggin' about the money he iss gonna make. By God!" Lauchie jumped to his feet. "He might be tryin' to run 'er now."

"But how did the Mountie get up in the woods?" asked Mary. "His car didn't come by here."

Nobody said a word, but Lauchie's agitation worsened.

"We best git a move on," he said, pacing to the door. "Maybe John'll git wise if he knows he iss headin' fer a trap. Maybe it's not too late to talk some sense into 'im."

Jim saw them to the yard, and returned. "We'd best git to bed ourselves," he said to Mary. "Lauchie wants to be in town early in the morning."

"In town for what? He just got groceries."

"Lauchie's cagey enough," Jim chuckled. "He's gonna give John a real strong warning tonight. But he ain't gonna be there to git nabbed in the morning. That Mountie's likely found the drum with the mash in it. Can't hide a thing that size, even in The Promised Land. Lauchie figures the Mountie's been watchin' fer around a week now. But he's got to catch somebody red-handed 'fore he can lay any kind of charge that'll stick."

"Why?" asked Mary.

"Because the way it stands, that mash could be the Beatons' or the MacTavishes' or anybody's at all. He'll not be able to prove a thing until he catches somebody tryin' to run it."

LAUCHIE AND JIM SET OFF for town before sunrise the next morning. At about nine-thirty the sun weakened, the sky grayed, and cold air blew in. Flakes of snow spiralled silently down until the sodden earth was covered. September was early for snow. It would be a long winter. Mary kneaded her bread and stared out the window as the heavy flakes levelled the fields, and the little brown hillocks whitened into strange mushrooms.

Her hand was raised to give the dough a final slap when she saw him—bounding towards the house. John MacTavish! His thin hair, matted with snow, fell in a fringe from forehead to twisted lips. His drenched clothes outlined his bones. His reddened hands jerked like flippers by his sides. He threw himself into the kitchen and leaned against the door gasping.

"Where iss Jim?" His voice cracked with terror and cold.

"In town with Lauchie," Mary's voice was calm and soothing. "They went early. I'm expecting them back any minute. But John, where's your coat and cap? You must be chilled to the heart. Sit down, and I'll make you some tea."

"Did ye see the Mountie go up?" John stayed standing.

"No!" said Mary, too loudly. "Is he up there?"

"He iss! I seed him through the window! Goin' into the barn carryin' the worm on his arm."

"Well, how did you get away? Weren't you with Dave? Did you leave Dave on his own? Where is Dave?" Mary's own voice cracked—with concern for Dave being left on his own and his mute attempts to deal with the Mountie's questions.

"Dan iss with him. Dan wouldna wake up. So I runned out the front door and comed through the woods. I thought Jim might be home and drive me somewheres."

Mary made him sit at the table and gave him tea.

Just then Jim's truck went past.

"There they go now," said Mary. "I wonder why they didn't stop for tea. Lauchie usually does."

"I gotta git outa here fast," squeaked John, jumping up and slopping tea on his shirt.

"Oh, sit down now. What would a Mountie want here?"

John tried the tea again, but he couldn't stop shaking.

Again they heard Jim's motor.

"There's the truck, now," cried Mary, relieved.

John jumped so suddenly he sent the cup flying across the table.

"I hafta git outa here." His face was ashen.

"It's stopped at the gate!" said Mary. "There's something the matter. Here! Get out the back—

take this cap and jacket."

She closed the back door on John, just as Jim came in the front. He was out of breath.

"Where's John? Is he here?"

"No! Not now. What's wrong? Did you run into the Mountie?"

"Yes!" Jim dashed to the window. "If John is anywhere around, get him the hell out. I know he came here. His tracks are plain as day. Can't think why the Mountie didn't spot 'em. He's in the truck now. Gotta take him back to the station. And the evidence with him."

"But what ev—?"

Jim waved off Mary's question.

"Told him I had to let you know where I was goin'. Tell ye about it later. Gotta go! He'll be gettin' suspicious. He's hellish cranky now."

JIM CAME BACK AT ONE O'CLOCK, and Lauchie joined him minutes later to mourn the day's mishaps. Gloomy over their failures, they needed to commiserate.

The Mountie, disguised in muddy wet mechanic's overalls and thoroughly peeved, had been waiting hidden inside the barn when Jim, hurrying back from town, drove up with Lauchie in the truck.

"What's your name?" he'd snarled at Lauchie, jerking open the door and thrusting his unshaven face into the cab.

"What iss it to ye?" Lauchie snarled back.

"What the hell's yer own name? And what's yer business in my barn?"

"That's not for you to question." The stranger was cocky, sure of his ground, demanding answers. "Where have you been?"

"Who in hell d'ye think ye are?" Lauchie's rising fury propelled him from the cab to stand facing the trespasser, fists curled.

"I am Constable Charles Adams of the RCMP, and I am looking for John MacTavish to arrest him." The Mountie spoke stiffly, biting off each word. His lips were blue. His outrage would have been obvious to a blind man. The legal situation was also obvious, but it had to be stated.

"What iss the charge?" Lauchie'd decided to tough it out.

"Distillation of liquor for the purpose of sale." The Mountie held up the coil and the bottle of tailings that had been in the barn for months.

"I knew we wass licked the minute I seed that bottle." Lauchie was shaking his head sorrowfully, unable to believe his bad luck. "Remember?" he turned to Mary. "I left 'er in the barn on the windowsill. Never went near 'er after the spring. Got too busy with the farm."

Mary nodded.

"He got the little funnel that joins the worm and the arm," said Jim. His voice was gloomy as Lauchie's. "Found it in Dan's pocket. He was a-sleep. Seized it fer evidence."

"But the damnedest thing of all wass—he

took my horse and wagon! He asked whose it wass. I said it wass mine and he seized it. Said it wass evidence." Lauchie's outrage was muted by the defeat in his voice. "He jist did that to be dirty!"

"How could he connect your rig to the mash? You weren't even home when he was searching?" Mary spoke with unusual heat.

"Last thing I told John 'fore I left the house wass to stay away from that rig," Lauchie muttered. "I knew that Mountie wass around, an' more 'n likely he'd spotted the place already. But, no, John iss too smart, y'know. He gits Dan to hitch up my horse—MY HORSE! and take Dave with 'im to move the mash. Wouldna go hisself—sent them. Now there iss a man fer ye! The Mountie'd been watchin' the mash all week—waitin' fer it t' finish workin'."

"Dan was caught too?" Mary gasped.

"Yi—sss!" Lauchie's hiss told Mary that Dan had been drunk. So blissfully drunk that he hadn't known what was going on.

"I hit every bump between here and town," said Jim. "But do ye think that arm or worm'd move. Oh no! Any other time, everything on the back would be flyin' into the woods. Not this time. He's got the evidence!"

"But, Jim, how did he get up there?" Mary was bewildered, and her questions tumbled out. "He never came by here after the night he got stuck and you got him free. And where was his car that you had to drive him to town?"

"He was in a sleepin' bag in The Promised Land the whole damn week. That night he said he was investigatin' the complaints about the sheep stealin'. Well, he was stuck in the bog just below where the little river runs across the road from The Promised Land. And he was sayin' likely whoever stole the sheep had gone up the river with them.

"Well, I knew he was tryin' to put one over on me, beingst I knew nobody up here had any sheep. So I just said that the thief would have a long way to go, since there wasn't a soul livin' near the river between here and Cromarty, and that's twenty miles up. That guff about sheep-stealin'! And it the middle o' the night in a downpour! But I shoulda been sharper.

"I never figured with all the rain that the river'd be high enough fer him to drive up to Cromarty and float a dinghy down to The Promised Land. It never got that high before, near as I can remember. But down he came with a little pup tent and a sleepin' bag, and enough grub to last him the week. He had lots o' time to look around. I never in my life seen a Mountie that determined before."

"My horse and wagon?" Two deep lines furrowed Lauchie's forehead. "I had no part in it. Can he seize my horse and wagon?"

"I wouldn't think so," said Jim. "But I don't know."

THE LAWYER IN TOWN knew well enough. Transporting Illegal Intoxicating Beverage was the offence. Dan was charged; Dave was too, though there was little chance of making him appear in court. Lauchie got a doctor's letter excusing him, just to make certain.

The Mountie got a conviction.

The blacksmith's wife wasn't summoned. John had disappeared, and she could testify only against him.

The horse and wagon were sold. Lauchie bought them back, but that was small comfort.

Jim got the forty-five-gallon drum, John's blackpot, and had it sawn in half. One half he used for watering calves; the other, for butchering hogs.

And so the matter ended—but not without lasting echoes. Another legend had been born. The MacTavishes made no more "runs."

John left the Glen and never came back. Mary wondered about the truth in the superstition that women around a still bring bad luck. And for years, the week of John MacTavish's blackpot, the week the Mountie had watched the still from his sleeping bag, remained a landmark for people to date happenings from. A kind of A.D.

The Year of Drought in The Promised Land.

The Day the Men Went to Town

WINTER WAS ANGRY even by Island standards. Ever since the first flurry of snowflakes in November, the winds had been busy shifting the drifts into strange shapes and forms, but it wasn't until after Christmas that winter really began. I hardly took the time to tie my shoes in the morning before rushing to the window to see what new pictures the night winds had drawn.

It was barely dawn and already Jim had shovelled his way out of the house, cut a path to the barn, the chicken house, the toilet and to the spring. In places the drifts had been higher than a man's head.

Jim sat now, taking long draughts of tea and staring at the list of groceries I had left on the table.

"Best get your pencil and start cutting," he said. There was no trace of resentment in his voice. "The Beatons and Lauchie must be out o' groceries, and your list will fill a whole sleigh."

"I can't cut much," I said, picking up the pencil. "We'll have to have flour—a hundred pounds, then with the potatoes and vegetables I canned we won't go hungry—as long as the meat holds out...we're out of baking powder...I can cut the rolled oats...lard? I suppose I could render some of the fat off the salt pork...matches...both kinds of soap...the dry beans can be halved, macaroni too. Ten pounds of sugar won't last for long, but I suppose it will have to do...salt...I can't cut any more. Heaven alone knows when you'll get out again. I'd better put tobacco and the papers down too, or you'll forget them." I pencilled in "one bag of candy," Jim could put that in his pocket. Jim never forgot to bring candy for the children, still it wouldn't do any harm to remind him.

"Bells!" said Jim jumping up from the table. "They're coming. On this of all days they have to come early. Must've started at midnight."

"Why are you in such a dither? Don't they always come early?"

"Yeh! But I ain't got that end of the road open yet."

"So what! They're early, you're late. There's no harm done."

"That ain't the point! I DIDN'T GET THE ROAD OPEN YESTERDAY!"

Jim's face was flushed with anger. "Time I got through with that whore of a shovel it was milking time."

"But there was a storm—you had a good excuse. They didn't come down on account of the storm."

"Cut it out, Mary, will ye!"

Yesterday had been a bad day. The blizzard had lasted for nearly two days. The temperature had fallen to five below zero. Jim had managed to cut a path to the spring to water the animals when the trouble started. The first bit of the shovel went deep into four feet of snow that covered the spring, but when he tried to pull it out heaped with snow, the handle broke just where it joined the spoon. Frost had made the wood brittle. By the time he had taken the stub out, taped the handle and set it back in the spoon, it had been time to feed the animals and clean the stables. It was too late to start opening the road. Jim had been ferocious. His hands had been stiff with cold, his frozen mitts had stuck to the metal shovel.

"Jim! Look! Harold's mare is in a drift," I shouted from the window. "They're all around him."

"Jesus! Jesus!" said Jim, fumbling with his jacket. "The only day in a month I missed opening the road, they have to come early. I'll be the shit of the Glen after this."

"Cut it out, Jim. A person would think the world was coming to an end all because you didn't open the road. Tell them about Silver. They'll not think it's your fault...."

"NO! They'll know damn well it IS my fault. Where's me mitts? It would have to be on MY stretch of road. Hurry! 'Fore they'll be telling everyone I sat in the house and wouldn't give them a hand!"

It was only last week that Silver had buried herself in a drift. I had never seen a frightened animal before. I watched the little mare writhe, her body covered with foam. I saw the spasms that shook her withers and her eyes full of tears. We took Silver home and led her into her stall. Billows of steam rose from her body; her eyes rolled with hysterics as Jim tenderly rubbed her down. I stood beside her talking gently into her ear as I stroked her foaming neck. It seemed hours before the drops of saliva stopped flowing—drops that turned to ice pellets before reaching the ground. Then we covered her with a blanket and bedded her down. Ever since that day I knew Jim would be reluctant to take Silver out after a storm.

Jim was running down the yard. Harold had calmed the mare with his petting. Jim started shovelling like a madman. In a few minutes the mare was free, and the little procession turned up the short road into the yard. Harold Beaton came first leading his pigeon-toed Queenie, straining at the huge stump hooked to the "swing" that packed the snow down hard and cleared a wider path than a log would have done. Queenie was the best snow horse on the Settlement Road because she was wise enough to stop and wait for Harold to shovel her out when the snow was too deep. Close behind her came Jennie, Joe Beaton's much-loved mare. Small, black, sway-backed, she drew a long log wrapped in logging chains. Last of all came Lauchie's big grey mare. Head up, nostrils flaring, proud and haughty, as though she pulled the fanciest of carriages instead of a homemade wood sleigh. "Them wood-sleds! Coldest things on earth. I'd be warmer walkin' in me shirt sleeves than bundled up riding on one o' them," Jim always said.

The men would be looking for tea! I prodded and turned the damp sticks in the range, trying to coax them to burn. I put out the cups and saucers and cut the bread. They were putting Jennie in the stable. Lauchie and Harold Beaton took their horses to the fence, tied and blanketed them there. "They must be taking two sleighs today," I said to myself.

The men pushed open the door and lumbered over to the stove. They took off their mitts and stood rubbing their hands in what little warmth they could find. There was little to distinguish the three men. Their long-billed caps with the fur-lined ear flaps hung over the collars of their jackets and their heavy woolen trousers ballooned out over their tightly laced boots like sausages.

"Devil take this place," said Jim as he closed the door behind him. "No phone, no lights, no plow, no nothin'.... Nova Scotia, the place God forgot!" Jim clasped his lips together as if he dared anyone to defy him.

"That's not true, Jim! The place God REMEMBERS is more like it. Next winter we'll have the plow. I've written to the Minister and to the engineer, and we'll have electric light and a telephone too, you'll see."

"That'll be the day!" said Jim, throwing off his coat.

"Breaking roads, now that all them farms is empty," said Lauchie, trying to cover up for my breach of good manners in "answering back" my husband. "Takes all a man's time in winter."

"They have to be opened," said Harold. "A single track anyway's, else it's 'good-bye.'"

"Going to town is an all-day job, all right," added Joe Beaton, taking his place at the table. "Even when there is a track." The men ate and drank in silence.

"Thank ye for the tea, Mary," said Lauchie, pushing back his chair and crossing over to the back door where their dripping jackets hung on a row of nails. He turned to Joe Beaton. "Ye be after going on my sleigh, Joe?"

"Me? Naw, I'll wait down at Dougall's. Harold'll be needin' a hand when he gets back. Thought I'd wait there."

Jim stopped and turned to me as he buttoned up his coat. "I don't know when we'll be back. Never mind the stables." Then he followed the men out and closed the door behind him. Jim knew, and I knew, that the stables would be cleaned before he returned.

I HOPE THERE WON'T BE ANY CALLERS. I have so much work to do and the day will be gone so quickly. The sun is a stranger most days now and it is a shame to miss a good day's drying. Will I ever be able to get the big wash and Sonny's diapers done as well? Not with all the outside chores...still I must try. It is a blessing that Joe Beaton is going to spend the day at Dougall's and not here, in my kitchen like he usually does. I hate washing diapers in front of a bachelor. How many times have I had to gather everything up in a rush and hide them in the pantry—any place to get them out of sight, when one of the Beatons or MacTavishes calls unexpectedly.

How shocked my sisters would be if they could see me now! A pile of dirty diapers on the floor—and they aren't all diapers either; many are pieces of worn-out undergarments salvaged from the rag-bag. My crooked old washtub standing on two chairs facing each other, seats touching. The family chamber pot in the centre of the room ready for the diapers after their first rough wash.

I put the washboard in the tub, then half fill a smaller tub with cold water, carry it over to the stove and pour in boiling water from the kettle. I balance it carefully on the edge of the stove and test the water with the other hand. It is just hot enough. Then I put it down beside the chamber pot and I kneel down. The little ones are playing quietly now in the other room, thank God! I wonder if Lauchie and the Beatons will stay the night? It will depend on how early they get back. If they stay, there will be four for cards and I won't have to play. I don't care much for playing cards, I'd rather watch, and when the time comes for tea I won't have to jump up between dealings to get things ready, or to keep the fire going. It's nice having company though. I get tired listening to the radio every night...the batteries are nearly gone, too...I'll have to order new ones on the budget plan...the bill at the store is too high to add any luxuries...if the weather doesn't break soon so that Jim can get into the woods for pit timber the store might stop our credit...but if the weather changes we'll be all right. God is good! How pretty Anne looked in her pink blouse...I was right...the colour brought out the pink in her complexion. "Pink wouldn't look right with her red hair," Clemmie said. But what does she know? Anne has the roundest, the bluest eyes I've ever seen...they dance with mischief and make you want to be a part of her fun—her laughter...Anne loves everything and everyone...and Sonny is so smart! Talking already...walking and running everywhere...no single steps for him...no single words either...from the very first it had been sentences...he is wise beyond his years, and it shows in his grey eyes...his little face must be startling to strangers...Sonny is so different from other children.

    I get up and stretch, to relieve the strain from crouching on the floor for so long. I'll have to dry some of the diapers on the line over the stove. I pick up the little tub of brown smelly water and carry it over to the door. I don't bother to put on my coat. It will only take a few seconds to throw the water out into the snow. That done, I pick up the big kettle of boiling water and stagger over to the tub. I pour the water, slowly at first, so as not to splatter and scald myself. I don't really mind washing, it gives me a kind of buoyance. I can feel the rhythm of the rubbing on the washboard...and my hands bobbing in and out of the water—it feels like part of a dance. The slapping together of the wet clothes, the swirling movement of the water, and the splatter of large drops when I lift a garment to cool, sounds like rain on a stagnant pool. I wish my back wouldn't ache so, and why should streaks of pain dart into my shoulders? No suds! And after using a whole bar of soap! The water is silent and dead; even with a tub of hot water I can't get a single bubble, the water is so hard.

I watch the last drop fall from the diaper; I twist it and stack it on the chair like cord wood. I swish my hand round in the water. There is nothing left to wash; my hand catches the side of the tub. That place is dangerous. Tubs don't last long around here. There are too many uses for them—Saturday night's baths, the washing and butchering. Jim had used this one to catch the entrails of a steer he butchered for Christmas. That is when it got bent. It will have to last until spring.

I don't know when the silence started. All at once everything is stifled, smothered, as if there had been a fall of goosefeathers so thick that I can't breathe. Silence in a house with children? That means mischief. I had learned that long ago. I kick off my slippers and tiptoe to the door and peer in.

There they are, the two of them, sitting on the floor close to the back wall; sitting in a circle of pieces of wallpaper—Anne's little hand grasping a frayed end still clinging to the wall and gently ripping it off the plaster board. I wanted to burst out laughing. Spanking them is hard but I have to do it or we won't have any paper left on the walls. I didn't really hurt them and they soon forget all about it and go on playing with their toys.

It had been fun to wash at home in Montana where clothes came out of the water gleaming white, but how can I get clothes white when the water is brackish and there isn't enough of it? Jim warned me to go easy because the water hole is going dry. He doesn't think there will be enough for the cows for another week, and Clemmie told me that she remembers when the people who used to live here had to take the cows down to the spring near the river in cold weather—and that is a whole mile away. The snow had to be cleared away before the cattle could reach the water and then someone had to stand by until they had finished drinking. Sometimes if a heavy frost followed a thaw, the cows couldn't cross the ice to get near enough to the spring to drink.

THANK HEAVENS! Only the rinsing to be done. I stretch my back again. What was that? A racket in the barn? It's noon already. No wonder the cows are complaining. All animals make a fuss when they are thirsty. I had better take a look. They'll have to wait for their hay until I feed the children and settle them down for their nap.

I put on my coat and rubbers and run down the yard. I throw open the door to the cow stable and brace it to the wall with a big stick, and step inside. It isn't until my eyes have grown accustomed to the half-darkness that I can see the burning eyes not two feet away. The bull! He must have broken out of his stall. And there he is standing behind the cows with a length of frayed rope round his neck. I can feel a constriction in my throat. My mouth is dry. I can't speak. I can't move. My senses come back slowly. I feel the pounding of my heart. Slowly I step back into the open doorway and quickly kick the prop aside and slam the door. What am I to do? I can't leave him there. Most of the cows are heavy with calf; they are wrenching at their chains, trying to free themselves. What can I do? I must try to get him back into his own stall beside Silver and across the threshing floor. I'll have to get behind him. But how? The only way is to crawl through one of the cows' feeding bins. Making sure that the door is secure, I run over to the "little people's door" cut in the big double doors that are only opened for the haymaking. The bull hears me and turns. Then he stands still and glares at me for a moment before pawing the gutter. Oh, God! Joe Beaton has stabled Jennie in the stall beyond Silver's, and if the bull passes his own stall and Silver's and reaches the mare, he'll gore her or she'll kick at him. Jennie'll kick at anything. She even kicks the boards of her own stall for want of something to do. I'll have to build a barricade of some kind to stop the bull passing his own stall, that is, if I can get him back that way at all.

There's a pile of old boards that Jim has left stacked in the corner. I pull out board after board. Thank goodness! Some of them are long enough to stretch from the wall to the end of the stall. But how am I going to support the boards? There is nothing but an old puncheon. I push and haul the puncheon over and use it as a brace. I slant some of the boards so that they slide in between the rails of the bull's stall. Perhaps the puncheon will keep them in position. It's heavy enough. Jennie is getting restive now, pulling at her halter and stamping her feet. Then she kicks with both of her hind legs. The beating of hooves against the walls of her stall sounds like thunder, but my barricade holds in spite of the shaking posts that anchor them. Now I'll have to reach the far side of the bull. How can I manage that? I could go outside and climb in through the little dung window...crawl through on my belly and then drop to the floor. No! I couldn't do that! There's another way. I can crawl through into a feeding bin in front of one of the cows, slide past her to reach the gutter. I walk down the length of the barn, passing each cow. Which stall shall I try? Star's? Poor gentle Star. Jim says she's so gentle that "she'd feel terrible if she even bumped ye!"

I open the clapper and look in. There's Star, but her eyes are now fiery and her nose so huge that a piece of paper couldn't be squeezed past. Perhaps I can get past one of the calves. Their horns are shorter. I run down to the other end of the barn. A pitchfork would be useful! I had better take it along. I can use it to drive the bull—if I ever reach him. I open a clapper to the calves' stall. Calves these animals might be, but they are spring calves, half grown, and now they look as big as elephants. I drop the clapper and look at my watch. The men have only been gone a few hours, and it might be seven or eight o'clock before they get back. I lift the clapper again. "Talk! Talk! Talk!" I say to myself. It will keep your teeth from chattering...take a deep breath...stand still until you stop shaking. Now! Open the clapper, stick the fork through first... leave the handle sticking out so that it will hold the lid up a little...now, first one leg...that's it...up and over...now bend down and put your head in. Quick! Squeeze your body through...hold your breath... there isn't much room but the calf's as far over as he can get...he looks frightened...he's in shock...but watch him...watch him. Why didn't I put the button on the clapper to hold it up...too late now... MOVE...keep going...look out! The calf! He's coming out of shock...quick... grab the fork...hold it before his eyes...go on...go on...the other foot...keep looking at the calf...he's getting bolder...he's getting MAD! Hurry! Hurry! Your feet are dangling... what's caught? Oh, Lord! His eyes are rolling now... I can't move...it must be my coat...take your mitts off...they're too thick, darned too much...I can't feel anything...the calf is edging nearer...Oh, God! If only this awful noise would stop...my hands will have to work...all those cows bellowing like cattle driven to the stockyards back home...that's got it! I'm free! Oh...the fork is stuck in a board...my weight must have driven it in...it's jammed...the calf is coming nearer....

I can't remember how I pulled the fork free and got through the stall. My memory didn't start working again until I found myself in the gutter with the bull. As soon as I passed him the calf started a wild twisting tantrum, pulling at his halter and roaring. Another second and he would have killed me. Now Daisy is frisking! I should have remembered that Daisy was due. It was she who brought the bull over. If only I had remembered I could have left the door opened, untied Daisy and driven the two of them out into the yard. They wouldn't have bothered anyone. It's too late now, I can never crawl back past that calf.

Holding the fork before me I inch my way along the gutter behind the twisting bellowing cows. The bull turns his head and looks at me. I jab the fork straight at his rump. He jumps and turns to face me. I jab again, this time at the neck, but in order to get a straight jab, I have to back into Daisy's stall because of the length of the fork handle. Daisy is incensed and lashes out with her hind leg. I feel pain tear through my knee...again I strike the bull. Slowly and very independently he turns and moves forward in the direction of his stall. Once he starts, he keeps going until he reaches the treadway at the end of the barn and without prompting turns onto the threshing floor. I follow close behind, jabbing him every now and then to keep him moving.

Reaching the centre of the threshing floor, he becomes aware of the space around him, or perhaps because he doesn't like being pushed around, he turns suddenly and faces me. Fortunately the manure shovel stands within my reach. I grab it with my left hand and by holding it near the heavy end I find I can manage the fork in one hand and the shovel in the other. Still jabbing with the fork I raise the shovel before the bull's eyes...he moves forward...I sidestep...he moves forward...I jab again...I don't want to give him time to think or brace himself for a charge. At last I have him facing in the direction of his own stall.

Then without warning he lets out a wild roar that shakes the barn to its foundations. He lowers his head and begins dragging his hoof slowly across the ground. With a crack like a pistol shot he strikes his own belly. I watch him helplessly. Without thinking I drop the fork, scoop up a pile of hayseed from the floor and throw it into his eyes. Then I pick up the fork and run across to a short ladder that leads up into the hay loft. The bull is quiet now. He shakes his head and blinks his eyes. I pull off my coat and drive the fork through the collar again and again, pleating the cloth to prevent it from slipping off the prongs. Then I lower it and the coat, fluttering like a pirate's flag in front of the bull at the entrance to his stall. For a moment he looks at the fluttering coat with indifference, then, as if he had just found his enemy, he lowers his head and charges. As I had hoped, the momentum of his charge carries him into his own stall. I drop the fork, scramble down the ladder and grasp the shafts of the hay rake that stands at the head of the threshing floor. I pull the unwieldy machine across the entrance to the stall. The cows are safe!

I kneel down and crawl underneath the hay-rake to retrieve my coat. I am shivering now, and exhausted. I lie there for a minute to rest, until my breathing becomes more regular. I soon find the machine over me oppressive, and besides, my nostrils are full of dust. I crawl out, brush the hay from my clothes and put on my coat, then I close the barn door behind me and walk up the yard towards the house. The children are still playing quietly, they haven't even noticed that I had left the house. Thank God, I only have the rinsing left to do.

The Funeral

"Bells," said Jim, his fork poised between his mouth and his plate. "Got both teams by the sound of it."

"It's Harold Beaton and Lauchie, and they got Dave with them," said Mary, pulling back the window curtain. "Maybe they're goin' to the wake and they'll take me along with them."

"You've been sulking all afternoon," said Jim. "Can't see why you're so set on freezing yerself to death, for the life of me. It's not fit for a woman to be travellin' all them miles." Mary pretended not to hear.

"That grey mare of Lauchie's won't let him tie her," she laughed, "keeps nibbling at his arm looking for attention. He's got her spoiled. Can't be staying long, that's sure. They're tying the horses instead of stabling them. I'd better get the tea ready."

"Good evening," said Lauchie as he pushed in the door.

"Cummina Hashen!" It was Harold Beaton, right behind him. "She's cold. Snow comin' down till ye can't see a hand ahead a ye, an' pilin' up."

Dave touched his cap and nodded to Mary as he closed the door behind him.

"Did ye have any trouble gettin' down," said Jim. "I was up to the wake yesterday, never seen so much snow."

The men took off their mitts and stood over the stove rubbing their hands. Except that Harold Beaton was taller than the MacTavish brothers, there was little to distinguish the three men.

"Ye wouldn't have any t'bacco, would ye?" said Lauchie, looking hopefully at Mary, "all of us 'up' are out." Mary smiled and took down a packet from the shelf by the stove.

"We thought, maybe, if ye was goin'," said Lauchie, "we could take the three teams, Jim, but I suppose being ye was there yesterday, ye won't be going tonight? Travellin' would be easier with the three teams."

"You can't get HIM to go again," said Mary. "I've been trying all day to talk him into taking me up. I baked a whole ham shoulder and other stuff, special, and now I can't get them over. I wanted to stay the night with the remains, too, for old Sarah's sake, poor old soul! She's going to be lost without Tom. They were close."

"I've been tellin' her she's crazy, in this weather," Jim shook his head. "Be different if it was summer, but to go all the way there on a sleigh? She'll freeze, mebbe be stuck in a snowdrift two, three hours. Sarah won't be expectin' her in this weather...."

"Nooo!" said Lauchie, slowly. "I don't s'pose they'll be expectin' many." He took a quart bottle of bush whiskey from his hip pocket. "I've got a little sip here. If ye'll git a little glass, Mary, ye can put 'er around. Ye're welcome to come with us, being we're going."

"Thanks, Lauchie," she said.

Mary filled the glass three times, standing before each man until he had swallowed his drink. Then sat the bottle and the glass down on the table. "I'm goin' to get Dave a cup of tea and get ready," she said. "If you fellows want any more, help yourselves."

When Mary returned the men's voices had grown louder. They were discussing the weather.

"You remember, don't ye," said Lauchie, "winter b'fore last, when Dan held up that long strip of guts from the pigs and said there'd be no snow to speak of."

"He musta been lookin' at the wrong end," said Harold. "I remember the old man up used to hit her every time."

"That's only a story the old-timers made up," said Jim. "Didn't Dan hold up the gut and say we'd have no snow till March the year he butchered here? The next day it started snowing an' never let up till April. You remember, Mary?"

"I didn't see it. I never go near when there's butcherin'." Mary dropped an armful of blankets on the floor.

"I'll guess it'll be pretty rough gettin' to Tom's," she said, tying a scarf over her head. "Didn't they tell ye at the wake, Jim, that the man on the plow told Father Mac he wouldn't take the plow out for him?"

"Got real nasty, they said." Jim nodded his head.

"He'll not be sitting on that plow next year," said Lauchie. "Ye can bet on that! Father won't be taking no guff from the like of him. Did they get the road open?"

"Father Mac called the engineer," Jim went on, "but the plow didn't show up before I left yesterday. Father went up on Willie MacDonnell's sleigh. They broke road most of the way with Willie's double team. One time the horses went in up to their necks, I guess, and Father and Willie had to work like bastards to get them out."

"Every one in the parish should write that engineer. Wake him up. You think! Refusing a PRIEST, and talking disrespectful to him's bad enough, but not even opening the road for to save a poor man's soul. I wouldn't want to be in that feller's place. No sirree!" said Harold.

"If she's that bad travelling, we'd best get moving," said Lauchie, looking at Mary. "Ye ready?"

LAUCHIE'S MARE, a cool-headed animal, good in snow, took the lead. Harold kept his sleigh close behind at first, then let his pigeon-toed mare, Queenie, make her own pace. She lacked the endurance of the grey. Mary travelled with Harold. They hardly spoke. They watched the mare straining in the traces. Ahead, Lauchie had reined in and was having a drink.

"Best get off and get your blood stirring," he said, as they drew up. Mary's hands and feet were so cold that they ached to the bone. In a moment they were all dancing little jigs and flapping their arms like wounded doves. But there was no time to lose. Soon the lanterns would have to be lit.

As they turned the bend in the road, Lauchie's mare plunged into a drift and sank up to her shoulders. The mare looked back at them, and Mary shuddered at the terror she saw in the animal's eyes. It was Harold who reached her first. He started to dig furiously. Lauchie threw himself at her neck and wrapped his arms about her head, like a hen straddling a nest of eggs. He cooed and carressed her as if she were human. Dave was shovelling so fast that his movements were blurred.

"Here, let me hold her head and keep her quiet," said Mary, pushing her way through the drift. "You can shovel faster than I can." Mary's voice threw the mare into a frenzy.

"Get away from her, Mary!" Lauchie shouted, "that mare's scared of ye. She ain't never heard a woman's voice a'fore. For God's sake! Look at her. Froth foaming from 'er mouth and her gasping. She's near gone!"

"If ye can shovel, Mary, grab that shovel of Lauchie's," Harold yelled, "and try to get her side cleared there. Perhaps she'll calm down some."

Mary was strong, and she shovelled with a will.

"Get off her head," Harold shouted, "let her see she's near freed in front."

"There, there, girl," Lauchie cooed, as he rubbed his coat sleeve across his eyes and slid down her back. He snatched the shovel from Mary and pushed her aside. The mare, sensing her freedom, strained forward and back. Then, as if by magic, her eyes were calm and her breathing easy. She stood quiet and rested.

The men dug feverishly, trying to release her hind legs before she tried to free herself again, but the mare, feeling the snow loosen, shied, then lunged forward. She tore off down the road dragging the sleigh behind her. One of the traces broke under the strain and waved like a streamer in the breeze. Lauchie moaned as he watched her, too stunned to make any effort to follow.

"Come on!" Harold yelled, "jump up. We'll get Queenie through the drift in the grey's tracks. Come on! Get up!" Lauchie crawled aboard like a sleepwalker. There wasn't even a drink to give them. The bottle was on the other sleigh.

About two miles up the road they caught up with the mare. She had run herself out. Lauchie looked her over carefully, and gave her a few strokes and a pat, then went over to the sleigh for some whiskey. Disregarding his manner, he pulled the cork and tipped the brown jug into his own mouth, then passed it to Harold. Then the two set about mending the trace.

"There's a halter rope by the shovel on my sleigh, Mary," said Harold, "will ye get it?"

"Perhaps she'll hold as far as Tom's. We'll do an all-right job on her there."

"No moon tonight," Harold observed. "We done good to get here when we did."

THEY REACHED TOM'S PLACE shortly before nightfall. The men went at once into the little room and knelt beside the coffin. Rising from their prayers, they turned to old Sarah, who sat, beads in hand, in an ancient rocker at the head of the coffin. Her gentle face bore no mark of tears or agitation, but the handkerchief in her hand had been squeezed into a tight ball. Solemnly the men approached her.

"Cummina Hashen!" said Lauchie, "I'm sorry fer your trouble, Sarah." The old lady looked at them gratefully. A smile touched the corner of her mouth, but she didn't speak.

"Cummina Hashen!" said Harold in turn, "I'm sorry fer your trouble." Dave grasped the old hand, crossed himself, sucked in a long breath, then nodded respectfully and followed Harold and Lauchie to the wooden bench placed along the wall.

"Good night!" said Lauchie, addressing Sarah's three nephews, seated beside him, "bad weather we're havin'."

"Yeh!" one answered, "hev to bury the old man tomorrow, no matter what. We was thinking perhaps some of them would get home. First thing after we heard they couldn't make it the weather got bad. Almost a week now. Good thing she's been cold. How'd ye find the roads?"

"Well, now, she'll be jist hard enough, getting the remains to the church," said Harold, looking over to the bench along the opposite wall where Hector Baines sat beside Dan MacTavish. They were settled for the night.

The small table at the foot of the coffin had been draped with a cloth of fine lace. In the centre had been placed the family Bible in silent petition to the Almighty for the repose of Tom's soul. The brown leather cover, encrusted in an intricate floral design and etched in gold, caught the flickering light from the candle standing in a tall white holder. Ranks of Mass cards covered the rest of the table, standing like supplicants and open for all to see the names of those they represented.

The coffin was open. The body lay in state. The hands were folded across the chest and clasped a prayer book entwined with a rosary. A tall crucifix stood at the head, and at the foot a small kneeler covered with worn carpeting. Father Mac had brought them on Willie's sleigh. The lid of the coffin stood like a silent sentinel against the wall behind the crucifix. The odor of death weighed the air.

"Hello!" said Dan. His eyes were so heavy he could barely look up from the floor to greet his uncle.

"Ye been here long?" said Lauchie.

"Got here last night, me and Hector come on

the wood sleigh."

"Cummina Hashen!" Hector stood up and pushed himself between the brothers, throwing his arms about like a spider trying to overpower a fly, his black eyes unfathomable under his heavy black eyebrows.

"Ye old son of a whore! Ye wouldn't have a little drink, would ye? Me and Dan is near dead," he concluded in a whisper.

Lauchie's face flushed as he glanced at old Sarah. Sarah hadn't heard a word.

"What makes ye sick?" asked Lauchie noncommittally.

"Young Tom, there, had a jug. We drank her last night between the three of us...ain't had a bit to eat today. Me and Dan's been too sick to look at anything. Ye got just one little taste?" Hector coaxed.

Lauchie didn't bother to answer. He shook off the encircling arms, bent down and whispered to his nephew. Dan's face lit up like a child's on Christmas morning. Together they left the room. Hector followed uninvited.

MARY LEFT HER BOX OF FOOD in the kitchen, took off her coat, put on an apron and came in to pay her respects. Tears came to old Sarah's eyes as she saw Mary kneeling beside the coffin. "Mary, Mary, 'tis good to see you," she said, holding out her arms to the younger woman.

"I'm sorry for your trouble, Sarah," said

Mary, clasping the thin veined hands in her own. "I was talking to Annie in the kitchen. She said she arrived last night...were you surprised?"

"Yisss!" old Sarah smiled, "I was that happy to see her. Don't know how we could have managed if she didn't come. Jennie MacNeil, beautiful soul that she is, come and stayed over...we'll never be able to do enough for that woman."

It was said of old Jennie that a touch of her hand and a willow'd stop weeping. She smiled at Mary, showing her few scattered teeth, as she busied herself preparing the tea. Her straight grey hair was drawn back so tight into the bun at the nape of her neck that it seemed hard for her to close her eyes. Jennie didn't walk; she glided silently about on the hem of her dress. She was always barefoot—winter and summer. She possessed three dresses, all cut from the same bolt of coth— navy blue cotton with an all-over pattern of pink roses. The tight bodice, securely buttoned up the front, seemed to apologize for the voluminous skirt which reached down to her ankles. The grey shawl, which she wore outdoors, lay carefully folded on the back of her rocker. Many years ago she had spun and woven the cloth herself.

"I'm staying the night, Sarah, least I can do," Mary said. "It'll give Annie a chance to rest up for the funeral tomorrow. Jennie's staying too. I'd best get back to the kitchen, but I'll be back."

MARY HADN'T FOUND IT EASY to reach the

kitchen. The men had gathered in the hall. Sean had arrived!

"Look, Mary," said Hector holding one of Sean's snowshoes in his hand. "Ever seen Sean's snowshoes? Ten-twelve miles from your place, ain't it, Sean? Wearing out the only snowshoes in the county, an' two horses in need of exercise, gittin' stall fed in the barn. Scared they'd mebbe be losin' their shine? Sean keeps 'em shined up all the time."

"Gimme that snowshoe!" Sean's eyes were blazing. "Set me back twelve dollars. NEW. Ye'd best be mindin' yer own business, if ye have any. Legs is made for walking. Yez're all jealous of that team of mine. Way some of you treat yer horses ain't fit for a dog. Taking them out in all weathers, burying them in drifts and driving them till they looks like calves that's been after sucking and the froth still slobbering out of their mouths. Git outta my way!"

"Someday," Hector snapped, "they're gonna pick ye up in one of them snowbanks and them horses home won't be after eating oats then!"

The men stood back and let Sean go by to pay his respects. Not one smiled until he had gone through the doorway, then they all burst into a roar of laughter.

After allowing time for Sean to say his prayers, Lauchie went into the room, took him by the arm and led him out for a drink. The incident was over and forgotten.

The little parlour was dark now and Annie

brought in a lighted lamp and placed it on the table beside the candle.

"We'd best be gitting under way," said Lauchie signalling to Harold, "the wind's comin' up, and she's dark."

"Ye can't go yet!" said Annie, "supper's on the table. Ye can't leave without a bite to eat. C'mon, Mama, there's room fer all." Annie led the mother out into the kitchen and sat her down at the head of the table. "The rest of ye just sit wherever ye find a place," she said.

"Will ye be stayin' the night, Sean?" said Mary as she placed his tea before him.

"I suppose me old legs ain't likely fit for to carry me another twelve miles this night." Sean had a twinkle in his eye. Sean always stayed.

"Guess Dave'll be staying too," said Lauchie, who had overheard, "least ways that's what he was tellin' me in the room."

"You and me, Mary'll, stay up with 'em," said old Jennie as she filled the cups.

"There'll be just four of them," Mary answered, "Sean, Dave, Hector, and Dan, and there's plenty cooked. All we'll have to be getting them is breakfast."

"Well!" said Lauchie, pushing back his chair, "I guess we'll hav' to do like the beggar, and get going...no moon at all."

"Did ye bring lanterns?" said Sarah, her voice quivering with concern. "I hate to see ye leaving on such a wild night."

"We'll be all right, Sarah," said Lauchie, grabbing Harold's arm. "Come on, we'd best say some more prayers and git under way."

The two men hastily left the room. Hector, Sean and Dan gulped down their food and followed. Lauchie and Harold were just leaving. Dan grasped Lauchie's arm and whispered in his ear. Lauchie didn't look too pleased, but nodded. Without bothering to fetch his coat Dan followed him out into the yard. A few minutes later he returned, shivering with the cold, but smiling. Hector mouthed a question. Dan nodded his answer, and both men went happily into the little room to watch beside the remains.

"Will somebody lead the rosary?" said Annie. "Mama's tired, and all of us are going to bed, so's to be rested for tomorrow." Then turning to one of the nephews she said, "Young John, will you lead?"

"Ach! no Annie," he mumbled, "git someone else. I'd come out two or three beads long or short, and I don't know the mysteries."

"I'll lead, if you want me to," said Mary.

When the lumbering sounds of kneeling men, clearing of throats and coughing had ceased, Mary began. When it was all over old Sarah took a last look at the coffin.

"Good night," she said softly. "If any of you get cold or sleepy during the night, there's a cot in the store room across the passage. Look and see if there's a blanket, Annie."

"Quit worrying, Mama," said Annie, tugging

at her mother's arm, "there's a blanket. Come on to bed, now."

Soon the family had all gone to bed and only the night-watchers remained downstairs. Old Jennie threw herself down on the bench beside Sean. It was the first time she had taken a rest that day.

"So!" she said, "ye walked all the way over in yer snowshoes, eh? First thing we know ye'll be after getting yourself a wife." Sean squirmed, then smiled.

"Far's that goes, I could probably show these young fellers a few tricks yet." And he raised his arms as if to hug Jennie.

"I'll just bet you could, too," said Jennie drawing back, "I wouldn't chance ye anyhow. Would ye, Mary?"

"Oh, if I come around, just once," Sean bantered, "Jim and Angus might as well pack their suitcases...the two of ye'd never look at them again."

"What've ye got, Sean," said Jennie, "must be yer hiding it!"

Sean moved his hands towards his fly, "Ye really want to see?"

The woman's screams and laughter roused Dan and Hector from their own conversation.

"You'd had best watch out," Hector said, "Sean's a gay old dog. I heard say as how ye had the girls all following ye around in your day, that right, Sean?"

Hector didn't wait for the laughter to subside

but threw his arms around Dan. "C'mon, Comrade Comfy, open her up! Open her up! Where's ye have it?"

"I have it in the storeroom beyond," said Dan, brushing off Hector's embrace. "Didn't wanna bring her in with the others around."

"Get her, man! Get her!" Hector pushed Dan up from the bench.

"Have ye a glass, Mary? A water glass. Them little devils don't hold a taste."

"Ye'd best be careful with that bush whiskey," said Jennie sternly, "be something fearful if Sarah got up and ye was all after passin' out."

"Ye'll likely be laid out with the remains, come mornin'." Mary laughed as she left the room.

"Well!" said Jennie, looking down at old Tom, "Mary an' me don't wanna be sittin' up alone with no remains, I'm tellin' yez. What's ye think of old Tom? Looks good, don't he? Except maybe he's got small."

"Fell away 'til there ain't a pick on him," said Sean, his eye on the door, "looks like an old dried-up herring in a cart box."

"There's a cot in the storeroom across the hall," Jennie said, quickly changing the subject, "with an army blanket spread over it. There's a bunch of junk in there, everythin' piled here and there, so ye'd better take a lantern—if one of ye wants to sleep."

"You put her around, Jennie," said Sean rubbing his hands when he saw Mary coming in through the door, "take one yerself and give one to Mary."

Jennie and Mary accepted the customary woman's sip.

"Now, make her a good one," said Hector, as Jennie filled and refilled the glass until they had all had a drink. "Dan, we'd better have another, hadn't we," said Sean, lowering his drink as if he were in a desert. "Can't walk on one leg y'know."

The glass was passed round at five-minute intervals four times again. Dave fell asleep immediately, and Sean began his first story.... "Speaking of the remains...had a jug of that old black rum we used'ta get for a dollar a gallon...every one was after feelin' good, an' lookin' for some devilment for to pass the night...sittin' up with Harry and the Rooster's remains he was...."

MARY LOOKED HELPLESSLY AT JENNIE.

"No need us listening to them. She's cold in here. Let's you and me get to the kitchen where it's warm." The men didn't seem to notice the women's departure. Out in the kitchen, Jennie turned the lamp down and drew her chair close to the fire.

"Put yer feet in the oven, Mary, get them out of the draft. We'd best get some sleep," said Jennie, pulling her shawl close about her. It was midnight.

"Get's creepy in the middle of the night, doesn't it?" said Mary shivering. "Sitting up with a corpse."

"Your first time?"

"Yes!" said Mary peering into the shadows. "Awful quiet."

"Yeh!" Jennie yawned. "Not even a pigeon cooin'."

THE WARMTH OF THE FIRE was comforting: against her will, Mary began to feel drowsy. She woke with a start.

"Jennie! Jennie! Wake up! Did you hear that noise?"

"What's up?"

"I heard a door banging or one of them fell down, had I better take a look?"

"One of the guys steppin' out to take a piss most likely," said Jennie, shifting her weight in the chair. "Sit still or ye'll be having 'em on our necks the rest of the night."

Mary made no comment when she heard other noises in the front of the house, and very soon both women had fallen asleep. It was Jennie who woke first.

"Mary! Wake up, it's three o'clock. It's time to make the tea. The men'll think we're fine housekeepers. Funny they haven't been lookin' for it!"

"They don't know if it's night or day by now," said Mary, stretching herself.

"Let's take the tea in to them, if they come here and see the fire we'll be listenin' to their gab till breakfast time."

"Suits me," said Mary, picking up two mugs of steaming tea and a plate of bread. Together they filed down the narrow hallway into the parlour. They looked round the room.

"Where's Dave?" said Mary.

"Gone over to sleep in the cot more'n likely. Maybe that's what ye heard before." Neither thought to wait for one of the men to answer. Hector wasn't in much shape to answer anyway. He held his bread in an unsteady hand and spilled the tea. Dan was fast asleep. But Sean's eyes were as alert as ever. He took his tea without mishap and ate hungrily. Returning to the kitchen the women washed and put away the dishes, put wood on the stove, and again drew up their chairs to the fire.

"We'll have to wake them up after a while," said Jennie, as she put her feet back in the oven. "Father Mac'll be here for prayers at seven sharp...came as far as O'Donnell's last night."

"Let's not wake 'em earlier than we have to," said Mary, trying to snuggle down into her hard wooden chair, "that Hector'll drive me crazy. He thinks all ye has to do is say some magic words and there'll be a drink for him in your hand. If there's vanilla or shaving lotion around we'd better hide it before waking him."

IT WAS FIVE-THIRTY when they woke. Jennie jumped up with a start.

"Mary! Ye awake? We'd best get the men from the room and feed them. Perhaps they'll go some place and sleep while we fix the room."

"You're right," said Mary pushing back her

chair. "It wouldn't be nice for Sarah to see Dan asleep in there and maybe a puddle under him, and heaven knows what shape Hector is in by now."

Together they went down the hall.

"May the Good Saints preserve us!" said Jennie on the threshold, blessing herself hastily, "will ye look at this!"

Cigarette butts, tobacco, chewed out tobacco cuds covered the floor. The puddle that the women knew they'd find under Dan's chair reached the rim of Sean's hat. Sean lay full length on the floor, his hat pulled well down over his ears. Dan was unconscious, but Hector had the brown jug tipped over his head, his mouth stretched wide, trying to catch the last drop. At the sound of Jennie's voice Hector let the jug fall with a crash to the floor. Then he too passed out.

"We'll never get this straightened out without help," said Mary, grabbing Dan by the shoulders and giving him a good shake. Dan muttered, crossed his legs, and slept on.

"Old Tom would turn over in his casket if he could see this mess," said Jennie, stepping over Sean to reach his feet. "You take the other leg, Mary, and we'll haul him out." Both women pulled with all their strength, but they couldn't move him.

"I'll fix him," said Jennie as she left the room. Mary sank onto an empty bench and surveyed the scene with desperation. Jennie returned from the kitchen with a pitcher of water.

"That'll fix him," she said throwing the water

over Sean's head. At that moment young Tom came running down the stairs. "What's goin' on in here?" he said, looking around the room. He did not wait for an answer.

"We'd best get Sean out to the fire afore he freezes. Can ye walk, Sean? Come on now." In spite of Tom's wheedling, Sean got to his feet only long enough to fall down again on a bench. He refused to go any further.

"Leave him, Tom," said Mary, "we can work around him. I'll get the mop and the water." Young Tom strode angrily out to the kitchen. One by one the family came downstairs. Old Sarah came down last of all. It was now half-past six.

"C'mon," said Annie, "Mama wants us all to say a prayer. Mary will ye start them off?"

Slowly they all filed into the little room and everyone but Sean and Hector knelt. The women reverently closed their eyes. The men stared ahead as if afraid it might appear effeminate to close their eyes.

"Our Father...," Mary began, "Who art in Heaven...." She got no further. A wild scream froze the prayer in Mary's throat. Dan leapt to his feet and was out the door before the echo of his voice merged with the howling and wailing of Young Tom and his cousins who followed as though swept up by a hurricane. The only men left in the room were Sean and Hector, both sound asleep.

"Heavenly saints!" Annie's voice was strangled in her throat, "is it that I'm losing my mind?"

Every woman in the room seemed to be turned to stone. In silence they watched a hand slowly rise from the casket, stop a moment, then slowly grasp its edge. They watched the skin whiten over the knuckles. Then slowly the top of a man's head...his forehead...and then the face. Annie reeled to her feet.

"Papa!" she whispered, and fainted.

It was Dave. The expression on his face told its own story. Dave thought he was dead. It was Sarah who grasped his shaking hand. There was no anger, no vestige of fear on her face. Her eyes were full of compassion for the poor fellow. She helped him scramble out of the coffin. It was her voice that calmed and reassured him. Slowly the fear left his face. Mary led the old lady back to her rocking chair and she calmly picked up her beads where she had left off. Mary turned to Dave.

"How'd you get in there? Do you remember anything?"

But Dave only grinned, hunched his shoulders and let them fall in bewilderment

"Twas Dave, dear," whispered Jennie, as Annie returned to consciousness. "Everythin's all right. Best sit beside Hector a minute."

Still uneasy on her feet, Annie sat down on the bench with a thump which upset Hector's balance, and without waking he slowly slid onto the floor.

"What have they did with the remains?" said Jennie, suddenly grasping all the implication.

"This is awful. We'll all be after going to hell. Belittlin' the dead like this."

She turned on Dave. "Did ye wake up after ye went to sleep at all?... Oh, what's the use. You don't know nothin'. It's them two slinks!"

Dave grabbed Mary's arm, and began making frantic signs. Mary couldn't make out what he was trying to say but nodded 'yes' and pointed to the door. Dave grabbed his cup from the floor and made for the door.

"I think Dave's gone for the men," said Mary, "now for those two hellions." She began to pummel Hector. "Come on you...Hector...wake up...come on now!"

"I'd best get after this old 'bodach,'" said Jennie, giving Sean a shake, "the old anti-Christ." She grabbed the pan of water she had brought to revive Annie and poured it over Sean's head. "There! That should fetch him, he's drenched good now!"

"Oh, me head!" moaned Sean. "What's wrong with ye women, leave me be!"

"Tell us where 'twas ye put the remains and ye can sleep forever," said Jennie harshly.

"Remains?" Sean blinked his eyes. "What remains?"

"Ye know what remains. Old Tom's, that's who we mean. No need ye sayin' ye don't know. Ye was telling about the night of the Rooster's wake when Mary and me left ye. Now where'd they hide that body?"

"Quit yer cacklin'," Sean's face became wrinkled with misery. "Me near dead with me sore head and all ye can do is rage about remains. Remains is in the box, far as I know."

"Wake up!" Jennie grabbed his shoulder and shook him, thumping his head hard against the wall. It was enough to make a "well" head sore. "We'll not leave ye till ye've told us, ye know."

Mary noticed that Sarah had finished her beads and had been listening ever since her hands became idle.

"Take your mother out for some tea," she whispered to Annie, "it'll do ye both good. No need for her to be hearin' all this."

"I don't know what we'll do." Jennie was near hysteria.

"I'll get some strong tea," said Mary, "that should do something."

"Bring a whole pot, Mary, an' we'll pour it down his neck till she's pourin' out his ears."

"The men's comin'," said Mary as she returned with the tea.

"Thet's somethin' anyways," said Jennie, taking hold of Sean's chin. "They can get Hector off the floor and search for the remains. Ye get on that other side, Mary, and hold his nose."

They poured one cup down Sean's throat and were starting on the second cup.

"Stop feedin' me that slop!" Sean spluttered, "ye're only making me dizzy and sick. Never remember like that."

The men came into the room.

"Put Hector back on the bench, fellers," said Jennie without looking up, "then spread out and try to find that body. Did ye see the clock when ye was in the kitchen, Mary?"

"It's half past six!"

"Mother o' God, Father Mac's due any time now. Get going." The men obeyed with unaccustomed docility.

"C'mon, Sean," Mary wheedled, "try to remember. Do you want the priest to see you like this?"

"Honest, I can't," Sean was almost in tears. "Good God! Woman, do ye think I'd hold her back if I knowed? An' the priest coming and all!"

"More tea," said Jennie sarcastically.

"NO!" Sean jerked his head clear of Jennie's grasp. "Please, Mary, if ye can get me a drop so's I can get me mind off me head, maybe it'll come back."

Sarah, beginning to show signs of anxiety, followed Mary back into the room. She had a pint bottle in her hand which she handed to Mary. Sean grabbed the bottle from Mary's hand and tipped it up. When he had half finished its contents Jennie snatched the bottle from his hand.

"All right, now, Sean," she said, "let's have it!"

"Holy God, Jennie, a man can't walk on one leg...'sides I didn't get enough to wet me throat good."

"That's every drop there is in the house," said Mary, going down on her knees. "We'll be hearing

Father Mac's sleigh bells any time now."

"WHERE DID THEY HIDE THE ROOSTER'S BODY?!" Jennie was desperate now. Mary snatched the bottle from Jennie's hand and gave it back to Sean.

"If this don't do it, I'd hate to be in his shoes."

"What in God's name are we goin' to do?" wailed Annie.

The sound of running feet and banging of doors came in from the yard, breathlessly the men entered the house and shook like sheep in a pen, huddled at the threshold. They shook their heads.

"I remember! I remember!" Sean said excitedly. "Me and Hector got the blanket from the storeroom and wrapped him in it. I recall almost dropping him a couple of times...kept slidin' on us."

"Yes, yes, but what'd ye do with him?" said Mary breathlessly.

"We took him across the hall to where the cot was."

The women looked at the men, who shook their heads.

"Ye didn't!" screamed Jennie, "the men looked. O God! I can hear Father's sleigh bells."

Slowly Mary rose to her feet and picked up the teapot and cup.

"Best get these things out of here, anyway."

Annie stood over the empty coffin wringing her hands. Old Sarah once again picked up her beads.

"Good God! Women!" said Sean. He was in his

dignity now. "Have ye got time to doubt me word? If ye'd let me talk instead of giving up and acting silly. The remains is there alright. Behind the door." Sean cleared his throat, "There's about a foot between the hinges and the wall, just enough as no one can tell when the door is open...now we stood him up...."

No one waited for Sean to finish. The sleigh bells rang out clearer now.

"Get goin'!" yelled Jennie.

"Mary! Look!" Queenie was near hysteria. "Dave tore the lining when he got out.... Jennie, get me a needle and thread, the lining has to be pulled together...the rip is where it'll show."

"Father Mac's at the gate," said Young Tom as they laid the body on a bench, still wrapped in the blanket.

"Stall him!" said Jennie as she hustled Tom out of the room.

"Hurry! Hurry! Get the blanket off him.... Sean, for God's sake, sit down some place," said Jennie, shaking her fist. "Tis prayers ye'll be needin' after this stunt."

"It'll have to do," said Annie, breaking the thread with her teeth, "bring him over and lay him in. Lookout! you've got him feet first...turn him around!"

"Quick! Quick! Father Mac's at the door!"

The men turned the body round clumsily. Mary held the sewn edge down as they laid the body in the coffin. Annie straightened her father's tie and replaced the rosary and prayer book in the folded hands. The door opened.

"Cummina Hashen!" Father Mac said as he entered the room.

"Everyone is ready for prayers, I see." The priest smiled. "Well, we'd better get started. It's a long way to the church." Everyone knelt. If some of the silent prayers were of thanksgiving and not those for the dead, the good Father never knew.

The six pallbearers walked beside the coffin every step of the six miles to the churchyard. The horses went down so many times that no one bothered to count the number. Old Tom was taken to his final resting place in his sleigh—the horses had been his too. The gravediggers, digging since daybreak, were still digging when the procession—horses and sleighs of all kinds—came round the bend, and the sun, weakened and weary, clung indifferently to the western sky.

ALSO AVAILABLE FROM
Breton Books and Music
(prices include GST and shipping)

- **THE GLACE BAY MINERS' MUSEUM**
  by Sheldon Currie
  While the ending of this book is shattering and unforgettable, Sheldon Currie's real contribution is excellent storytelling and the remarkable Margaret, an indelible new voice in Canadian literature. A passionate and compassionate novel set in the coal life of Cape Breton Island, this is a story that will reverberate and last. It is also a bizarre and marvelous book! **$16.25**

- **CAPE BRETON WORKS**
  More Lives from *Cape Breton's Magazine*
  From farm life to boxing, from lighthouse tragedies to fishing adventures, from hunting to mining with horses to work in the steel plant—this extraordinary mix of men's and women's lives delivers a solid dose of the tenacity, courage, humour and good storytelling that make a place like Cape Breton work. **$23.50**

- **A FOLK TALE JOURNEY THROUGH THE MARITIMES**
  by Helen Creighton
  72 folk tales from a lifetime of collecting. Dr. Creighton introduces each storyteller, then lets them talk to us directly, in their own words. Wonderful tales! A Maritime treasure. **$23.50**

continued on next page...

ALSO AVAILABLE FROM
Breton Books and Music

- **STERLING SILVER**
  by Silver Donald Cameron
  Rants, Raves and Revelations

  From over 25 years of extraordinary writing, never before in book form—*Sterling Silver* demonstrates Silver Donald's interests, compassion and fortitude. From suicide to love and fear, craftsmanship and community—this is Silver Donald angry, hopeful, incisive and amused. **$21.50**

- **ARCHIE NEIL**
  by Mary Anne Ducharme
  From the Life and Stories of Archie Neil Chisholm of Margaree Forks, Cape Breton

  Saddled with polio, pride, and a lack of discipline, Archie Neil lived out the contradictory life of a terrific teacher floundering in alcoholism. This extraordinary book melds oral history, biography and anthology into "the triumph of a life." **$18.50**

- **THE SEVEN-HEADED BEAST**
  & Other Acadian Tales from Cape Breton
  collected by Anselme Chiasson
  translated by Rosie Aucoin Grace

  These passionate, funny, bawdy and tender tales draw us closer to the heart of Acadian Cape Breton. Here's lively translations from the French of traditional storytellers Marcellin Haché and Loubie Chiasson, plus an introduction to their native Cheticamp by Père Anselme Chiasson. **$16.25**

ALSO AVAILABLE FROM
Breton Books and Music

- **GOD & ME**
  by Sheila Green

A gentle way of sharing questions and wonder and relationship with a child, and a lovely keepsake for any adult. 18 poems, with 7 tender drawings by Alison R. Grapes that nicely complement Sheila Green's open, unpretentious poetry. **$9.00**

- **CAPE BRETON BOOK OF THE NIGHT**
  Stories of Tenderness and Terror

51 extraordinary, often chilling tales, pervaded with a characteristic Cape Breton tenderness—a tough, caring presentation of experience. **$16.25**

- **ANOTHER NIGHT**
  Cape Breton Stories, True & Short & Tall

Some witty, some eerie, some heartrending, these stories convey the pleasure we take in entertaining one another. **$16.25**

- **SILENT OBSERVER**
  written, with 39 full colour illustrations,
  by Christy MacKinnon

Simply and beautifully told in her own words and paintings by a deaf woman who grew up in rural Cape Breton over 100 years ago, this children's book is a winning portrait of courage and good humour, and of family love. **$23.50**

continued on next page...

ALSO AVAILABLE FROM
Breton Books and Music

- **WATCHMAN AGAINST THE WORLD**
  by Flora McPherson
  The Remarkable Journey of Norman McLeod and his People from Scotland to Cape Breton Island to New Zealand

  A detailed picture of the tyranny and tenderness with which an absolute leader won, held and developed a community—and a story of the desperation, vigour, and devotion of which the 19th-century Scottish exiles were capable. **$16.25**

- **CASTAWAY ON CAPE BRETON**
  2 Great Shipwreck Narratives in 1 Book!
  Ensign Prenties' *Narrative* of shipwreck at Margaree Harbour, 1780. Samuel Burrows' *Narrative* of shipwreck on the Cheticamp coast, 1823. Notes by G. G. Campbell and Charles D. Roach. **$13.00**

- **HIGHLAND SETTLER**
  by Charles W. Dunn
  A portrait of the Scottish Gael in Cape Breton and eastern Nova Scotia. "One of the best books yet written on the culture of the Gaels of Cape Breton."—*Western Folklore* **$16.25**

...AND MUCH MORE!
Cape Breton Books • Music • Videos
• **SEND FOR OUR FREE CATALOGUE** •

Breton Books & Music
Wreck Cove, Cape Breton, NS B0C 1H0